The Curse
of the Lion People

Melissa Saari

Whimsical Publications, LLC

Florida

The Curse of the Lion People is a work of fiction. Names, characters, and incidents are the products of the author's imagination and are either fictitious or are used fictitiously. Any resemblance to actual events or persons, living or dead, is entirely coincidental.

If you purchased this book without a cover, you should be aware that this book may have been stolen property and reported as "unsold and destroyed" to the publisher. In such case, neither the publisher nor the author has received payment for this "stripped book."

To purchase the authorized electronic edition of *The Curse of the Lion People*, visit
www.whimsicalpublications.com

Cover art by Shyanne England
Editing by Brieanna Robertson

ISBN-13: 978-1-940707-98-3

Published by
Whimsical Publications, LLC
Florida

"Raino, please fetch some water for me so I can do the dishes."

He didn't want to go out into the dark night, but he wanted to make his mother happy.

"Yes, Mother," he said. Then he got a bucket from the corner by the door, put his boots on, and stepped out into the cold night outside.

Raino looked at the stars. They twinkled overhead, cold and very far away. He started to shiver. Both moons were glowing yellow in the night sky overhead; the bigger moon was bright enough to light his way out of the village to the well. Raino knew that he had to keep moving to make the shivering stop. He boldly trudged out into the gloom.

He looked back at the warm houses with their windows glowing gold from the candlelight. The roofs were composed of dried thatch, and in the dark night they seemed like frail protection indeed. In those long ago days, the windows were fragile.

Then he turned back and completed his trek to the well.

The well was made from stones hundreds of years ago. Moss glowed in between the cracks in the rocks. A rope hung over the well, with an old hook attached to the end.

Raino reached up and swung the bucket handle onto the hook. Then he started turning the old wheel, lowering the bucket slowly. It took a long time for it to reach the bottom. During this time, Raino got more and more nervous. He turned the wheel faster.

Finally, with a splash, the bucket reached the water and got heavier as the cold water spilled into and filled it.

Raino let out a long, slow breath of relief. He started turning the wheel the other way, this time with more effort because the bucket was full.

Deep in the forest, he heard an otherworldly scream. He looked up and let go of the wheel. The bucket splashed back into the well.

As he stared into the meadows, he could dimly see the shining grasses between him and the forest, while the black line of trees stretched from horizon to horizon, a wall of darkness at the edge of the cultivated lands.

Raino heard the fluttering of thousands of wings as more birds than he could count whooshed overhead, screeching a warning cry to the universe as they flew past him. Raino watched their silhouettes dance across the shining stars, and his fear was slowly transmuted into wonder as he stared at this dance, the wings flashing past the stars and making the sky glitter with magic.

Raino stared into the darkness, listening as rustling disturbed the grass before him.

He looked down at his feet and saw mice and squirrels and rabbits swimming past in a river of flesh—panicked, scurrying flesh. As wolves and other large animals began to crash past him, some missing him by a breath, he realized how much danger he was in. He saw a large elk running toward him, fully trapped in panic, with snot flying from his nostrils and foam flying from his wide-open jaws as it screamed in terror.

He flung himself to the side, rolling out of the way, and as more large animals stampeded past him, he stayed down. When the large animals were past, he watched them running through the fields, headed for the large mountain in the distance.

The discovery hit him with horror—they were heading for the high ground because something was chasing them!

He ran as quickly as he could for his home, screaming for his parents.

They came running out of their house, Father with his pitchfork and Mother brandishing a kitchen knife.

"Come see! There's danger out here! The animals are going for the higher ground!"

"What?" Father roared. "They only do that when they panic! This is bad!"

Raino's father grabbed a torch with his free arm, plunging the torch into a fire pit so he could use it to see and even drive away the threat, shouting for the whole community to hear.

"Villagers, get ready! Something's coming!"

Raino's parents hurried toward him, brushing him into their midst as they passed, because Raino felt safe with his parents by his side.

All the other villagers began to leave their houses too, answering the call, some lighting their torches in the burning barrels left in the streets, others grabbing as many pitchforks as they could carry and handing them out. They raced forward, into the night, trying to rally a defense as best they could.

As the villagers all crowded around, they felt the earth shake. They began to build up a stronger formation, a circle that kept the center highly guarded. As they prepared for the coming battle, they stared into the darkness, wondering what this shaking menace would look like. Each man was eager for the first glimpse, but the women silently prayed, far too wise to seek out the danger ahead.

Small lights danced across the meadows, a long line of red. Raino was mystified at first because the villagers used crude oil lanterns that poured out nothing but yellow light.

When the lights began to disappear and flicker back again, he realized they were eyes. As the eyes drew nearer, the rumbling became an audible groan as the earth shook, and soon the thunder of many strong legs pounding into the earth drummed across the landscape in a frantic staccato rhythm. He knew there had to be hundreds of legs hitting the ground, and too late his brain deciphered the threat before him.

"Monsters!" he screamed at the top of his lungs.

Acknowledgements

I would like to acknowledge all my teachers, advisors and editors that have helped me succeed on my path as a writer. I'd also like to acknowledge the teachers at Southern New Hampshire University, where I study screenwriting. Also, my dear friend Patricia McDonald, who has been a great support from the beginning.

Also by
Melissa Saari

The Red Satin Shoes
Blue Satin Diary

Curse of the Black Dragon (coming soon)

Mystic Lake (coming soon)

The Legend of the Pirate Queen (coming soon)

This book is dedicated to my dear friend, Alvin Golder,
who always makes me laugh

Chapter One

The Beasts

No humans stirred deep within the forest, for nobody ever dared to venture into the murky woods.

Beneath the sky, the meadows shone with moonlight, but in the forest, the thick green leaves of the trees hid the light of the heavens from the forest floor. Impermeable dimness surrounded the animals that called the forest home.

The rabbits burrowed into their nests quietly, and waited for dawn to come, while the owls hooted and the bats chirred as they flew through the air, collecting buzzing insects and avoiding the snoring wolves as the doves flew through the darkness.

A deep silence fell over the gloomy woods, from end to end, rolling like a wave.

The animals sensed something was wrong, and they all held their breath, waiting, while the silence became crushing, a presence that stifled the life of the forest.

A tenebrous murmuring whisper emerged from the blackness, a whisper that floated from tree to tree and filled the forest with a terrible cadence.

"Rise. Rise, my beasts, and go forth. Take back what belongs to you."

The animals were terrified, for even though they could not understand it, they sensed the evil in the voice and had enough wisdom to fear it.

A voice floated through the forest.

The foxes were frightened, but the strange swirling spirals developing in the earth panicked them even more.

They fled for their lives, running from the forest as fast as they could.

Elks trampled through the bushes and the wolves rushed through the undergrowth. They all knew that a great mountain lay beyond the forest, a place where they could reach the high ground and escape the threat. Behind them ran the foxes and the deer, and all the other creatures of the forest.

Smaller creatures scurried away as fast as they could, where they left many rustling leaves and cracking branches in their wake. Thousands upon thousands of squirrels and mice fled from the forest; with their tiny legs they made a slow ocean of movement through the tall grass and disturbed the low-hanging fronds on the ferns that blanketed the forest floor.

The owls flew from their trees, and the sparrows took flight, racing with the pigeons and the robins to escape the forest as fast as their wings could carry them.

The swirling spiral holes began to deepen into whirlpools, tearing the formation of the earth and ripping a tunnel through to another place and time.

From one of the whirlpools, thick swirling black smoke rose from the portal.

A huge black claw reached out of the hole and slammed into the dirt, making the earth shake. From this gigantic claw, a massive monster arose from the pit, dragging itself up until its other massive paw ripped into the earth.

The muscles on this beast were gigantic and writhing, and his eyes were red and dangerous. As he moved forward, the gigantic rent in the earth remained where his claw had struck the land of Santara for the first time.

Again the voice rang through the forest, as more monsters clawed their way to the surface after their leader.

"Rise, rise! Seek my book of dark magic. It will give me the strength I need to rule this land."

From these whirlpools, dark shapes crawled up out of the portals, red eyes glowing viciously and jet black hair making them nearly invisible in the darkness.

The wide portals quickly spiraled away, twisting back down into the dirt and returning the natural earth that once had been there. But where the portals closed, no living plants remained. Everything there had decayed and blackened, shriveling into death and collapsing to the forest floor.

The beasts wandered around in this new world, striding firmly, making tremors rumble through the dirt as their huge bodies connected with this new soil.

"Seek the edge of the forest, my children! There you can see for many, many miles. You can see all the way to my magic book. Go now!"

They all looked at each other, with eyes that could see clearly even in the greatest darkness, for these beasts could sense heat and smell flesh from miles and miles away.

Then, roaring, the massive beasts rumbled out of the forest, tearing through the trees and snarling and snapping their fangs at each other. Slobber hung from their jaws and whipped through the air as they ran. Their teeth were razor sharp from years and years of fighting. The ears of these beasts had also developed intensely, so their indented earflaps captured even the sound of the smallest scurrying mouse.

Following the scurrying of the terrified animals and the commands of their mistress, the monsters emerged at the edge of the forest, stopping and smelling the air ahead. Without a grunt or a snarl, they communicated, knowing it was time to regroup and gather intelligence.

As the monsters lingered by the edge of the forest, surveying the landscape and deciding their plan of attack, they deliberately sniffed the air with their powerful noses.

They yawned widely, tasting horses, humans, and grain-filled fields in the air. Their sharp eyes detected the body heat of villagers and animals, sensing many warm bodies scattered across the fields, and smelled the roasting fires from the castle, though it was way off across the meadows.

They clearly saw the distant castle in the bright light of the moons, and their heat-sensing powers found many people inside the cold walls.

Deep within the castle basement, their keen senses picked up a dark presence, protected by thick walls and heavy gates. The beasts were not threatened by these defenses, for they had torn through greater barriers. Given enough time, they could destroy the entire world of Santara, shredding every living thing in their path.

But they knew that their time in this world was limited, and for a single purpose—to reclaim the book that hummed deep inside the castle so the sorceress whom they served could regain her powers.

The book hummed with a deadly evil, and the hum that resonated across the meadows reached cavernous, sensitive ears. Sensing the dark magic and knowing where it lay, they only waited for their mistress's command, and it came soon enough.

Then they listened carefully to the whispers that once again emerged from the air.

"Go, my children! Destroy anyone or anything that stands in your path! Restore my book and my power and you'll never have to go back to that dark, dank, and vile realm of your origins ever again."

Then they began to run across the meadows toward the villages, their pounding feet making the earth rumble and shake.

Chapter Two

Raino

In one of the small villages near the dark forest, a boy named Raino lived with his parents. Raino was just a young teenager, skinny with blond hair, busy whittling a new fishing rod.

His mother, her apron embroidered with snowflakes and flowers, was finishing up dinner as she called to him.

"Raino, please fetch some water for me so I can do the dishes."

He didn't want to go out into the dark night, but he wanted to make his mother happy.

"Yes, Mother," he said. Then he got a bucket from the corner by the door, put his boots on, and stepped out into the cold night outside.

Raino looked at the stars. They twinkled overhead, cold and very far away. He started to shiver. Both moons were glowing yellow in the night sky overhead; the bigger moon was bright enough to light his way out of the village to the well. Raino knew that he had to keep moving to make the shivering stop. He boldly trudged out into the gloom.

He looked back at the warm houses with their windows glowing gold from the candlelight. The roofs were composed of dried thatch, and in the dark night they seemed like frail protection indeed. In those long ago days, the windows were fragile.

Then he turned back and completed his trek to the well.

The well was made from stones hundreds of years ago. Moss glowed in between the cracks in the rocks. A rope hung over the well, with an old hook attached to the end.

Raino reached up and swung the bucket handle onto the hook. Then he started turning the old wheel, lowering the bucket slowly. It took a long time for it to reach the bottom. During this time, Raino got more and more nervous. He turned the wheel faster.

Finally, with a splash, the bucket reached the water and got heavier as the cold water spilled into and filled it.

Raino let out a long, slow breath of relief. He started turning the wheel the other way, this time with more effort because the bucket was full.

Deep in the forest, he heard an otherworldly scream. He looked up and let go of the wheel. The bucket splashed back into the well.

As he stared into the meadows, he could dimly see the shining grasses between him and the forest, while the black line of trees stretched from horizon to horizon, a wall of darkness at the edge of the cultivated lands.

Raino heard the fluttering of thousands of wings as more birds than he could count whooshed overhead, screeching a warning cry to the universe as they flew past him. Raino watched their silhouettes dance across the shining stars, and his fear was slowly transmuted into wonder as he stared at this dance, the wings flashing past the stars and making the sky glitter with magic.

Raino stared into the darkness, listening as rustling disturbed the grass before him.

He looked down at his feet and saw mice and squirrels and rabbits swimming past in a river of flesh—panicked, scurrying flesh. As wolves and other large animals began to crash past him, some missing him by a breath, he realized how much danger he was in. He saw a large elk running toward him, fully trapped in panic, with snot flying from his nostrils and foam flying from his wide-open jaws as it screamed in terror.

He flung himself to the side, rolling out of the way, and as more large animals stampeded past him, he stayed down. When the large animals were past, he watched them running through the fields, headed for the large mountain in the distance.

The discovery hit him with horror—they were heading for the high ground because something was chasing them!

He ran as quickly as he could for his home, screaming for his parents.

They came running out of their house, Father with his pitchfork and Mother brandishing a kitchen knife.

"Come see! There's danger out here! The animals are going for the higher ground!"

"What?" Father roared. "They only do that when they panic! This is bad!"

Raino's father grabbed a torch with his free arm, plunging the torch into a fire pit so he could use it to see and even drive away the threat, shouting for the whole community to hear.

"Villagers, get ready! Something's coming!"

Raino's parents hurried toward him, brushing him into their midst as they passed, because Raino felt safe with his parents by his side.

All the other villagers began to leave their houses too, answering the call, some lighting their torches in the burning barrels left in the streets, others grabbing as many pitchforks as they could carry and handing them out. They raced forward, into the night, trying to rally a defense as best they could.

As the villagers all crowded around, they felt the earth shake. They began to build up a stronger formation, a circle that kept the center highly guarded. As they prepared for the coming battle, they stared into the darkness, wondering what this shaking menace would look like. Each man was eager for the first glimpse, but the women silently prayed, far too wise to seek out the danger ahead.

Small lights danced across the meadows, a long line of red. Raino was mystified at first because the villagers used crude oil lanterns that poured out nothing but yellow light.

When the lights began to disappear and flicker back again, he realized they were eyes. As the eyes drew nearer, the rumbling became an audible groan as the earth shook, and soon the thunder of many strong legs pounding into the earth drummed across the landscape in a frantic staccato rhythm. He knew there had to be hundreds of legs hitting the ground, and too late his brain deciphered the threat before him.

"Monsters!" he screamed at the top of his lungs.

The villagers noticed dark bodies swarming across the meadow. The light from the stars and the moons reflected cold and white against the black fur of the monsters' coats, dancing as the muscles bulged in tandem, hurtling them across the meadow with deadly speed.

Raino screamed as terror came out of every pore of his young body.

The villagers immediately went defensive, holding their pitchforks straight in front of them. The first monster slammed right into the pitchfork with his massive body, and the pitchfork lifted into the air. A second farmer impaled the monster at the same time, and they both brought the monster crashing to earth.

In the varying light of the torches, the monster was impossibly dark. Ink-black blood spurted from its chest and neck, and for a few seconds, it stopped moving. Then the red eyes blinked open again and the monster roared to its feet, tearing through the farmers that brought him down by swinging both of his gigantic forelegs at once, swiping their necks wide open and exposing every artery. Although Raino saw them die almost instantly, that one second seemed to last an eternity, both men hovering in place before crashing to the ground, spurting blood, but soon, even that stopped.

Raino turned to escape for the center of the circle, where he had the best chance of surviving. As he ran, he felt something slam against his side. Then there was a blow to his other side. A third monster came up from behind and he felt a blow to the back of his head. After that he didn't feel anything. He fell to the ground, eyes staring and already faded.

When the first monsters raced across the meadows, one of the women, Marisa, broke free of the circle and raced for the barn as fast as she could.

The barn was not far away, but it was away from the villagers, so she was able to get there without being noticed. She raced inside the barn, swinging the stall door wide open.

The horse inside was already scared, but Marisa calmed it down with soft clicks of her tongue. She knew it was her last chance to escape, so she wasn't about to lose her shot. Stroking the horse on its mane, she relaxed it enough to swing around and pull her bare toes up the side to ascend bareback.

Marisa felt light as a feather as she floated onto the horse, and the magnificent white stallion reared its head, surged out of the stall, and rushed out of the barn.

She stayed on the horse, expecting its frantic bucks, and kicked the animal in the gut several times with all her strength to get the stubborn beast on a solid run. She wanted the horse to move faster than lightning, faster than the red eyes sweeping closer to the villagers. Pushing on the horse's neck because she hadn't had time to grab the reins, she urged the horse away from the villagers.

The panicked horse raced on, not knowing the castle was its destination, only knowing that his rider wanted him to travel this way. Marisa's yellow hair flashed behind her in the moonlight. She knew she was the fastest rider in the village and the horse would bring her to the castle as quick as it could. They made a good team.

Marisa's heart was racing, and sweat was running down her face, even in the cold night.

Behind her, she heard the horrified screams of the villagers, and her heart pounded even louder in her ears.

She tried to ignore her own panic, but she couldn't ignore the weakness in her legs and the pain in her chest as utter fear took over her.

The screams of her friends tore at her heart; still she pressed forward, knowing she could do nothing to save the ones on the front lines, but she might be able to save some of the defenders if she could get help in time.

Her sweating grew more intense, and her body was wracked with pain as she heard the death throes of her friends. Some of the screams were cut off in the middle. She couldn't bear to hear their suffering, yet horse and rider crossed over a mile of fields before she couldn't hear them anymore. Then she squared her shoulders, turning her attention forward to the castle.

The horse made it there so quickly she had hope that some of her friends were still alive. It was just before the first glimmer of dawn, and she pounded on the door as hard as she could, hoping to wake whoever was inside.

The gate opened suddenly, and she was so surprised she tumbled headfirst through the gate, crying out as she fell.

"Monsters are attacking from the forest!" she screamed.

Chapter Three

The Commanders and the Knights

Eino was sleeping soundly in his chamber, just before dawn, when the guards pounded on his door.

"Prince Eino! Come at once!" shouted one of the guards. He heard others talking in the background, and knew something serious had occurred to bring more than one guard to his door before the sun even rose into the sky.

"Quickly! Wake the king and queen and we'll convene in the Throne Room."

When he reached the Throne Room, King Aro and Queen Agnes were there as well, and the guard who had awoken Prince Eino had brought a woman inside and stood by her nervously. King Aro was dressed in his armor already, as were Prince Eino and the two commanders that simultaneously crossed the Throne Room to his side the moment he strode into the massive hall.

He nodded to them, grateful that they found security in his presence, but his face remained taut and cold. He had chosen to bury his emotions on the way down the staircase, and was very glad he had done so when he saw the woman violently shivering as he arrived.

The messenger's tremors told him everything he needed to know about the coming danger. Whatever it was, it was very, very bad. He blessed his emotional fortitude again as he suppressed the fit of panic that tried to well up inside of him, forcing his stomach to cooperate and overriding the commands from his own brain through sheer willpower. Sealing the emotions deeper inside, he forced his face to hold the same blank line across his lips, the same cold steel glare in his eyes that he'd practiced so many times. Others in the Throne Room talked with each other, some muttering and some chattering.

"What's going on?" demanded the king. "It's not even daylight yet!" He drank strong, spicy tea and shook his head, making his magnificent braids shake from side to side, the priceless wrappings bearing the treasures of the kingdom to protect his sacred hair. They rattled against the armor, bringing silence to the entire room.

Into this silence, the wails of the messenger began to pour forth.

"Monsters attacked the villages by the forest during the night! I escaped to send the warning!"

"What kind of monsters?" King Aro inquired.

"Big monsters with black fur that bleed and still refuse to fall, my king."

"How many monsters did you see?" asked King Aro.

"Hundreds and hundreds of red eyes in the darkness," exclaimed the woman, and suddenly a huge gasp expelled from the people in the Throne Room, Prince Eino included. Beside him, Agatha and Aaroni tensed their shoulders, also knowing the truth.

"Red eyes can only mean one thing—that evil sorceress is afoot again! We have to do whatever we can to stop these monsters!" King Aro brought his fist down on the arm of the throne, half for emphasis and half for support as he pushed himself to his feet. The crash of his armored glove on the chair brought everything to complete silence. Even Agatha and Aaroni held their breath.

When King Aro stood up, his shining armor clattered and settled around his arms. The echoes fell away into the silence, but everyone still heard the king's labored breathing.

Then he broke out in a roaring cry.

"It is my duty to protect the Kingdom of Santara! My army will not stand by as my people are slaughtered! Hear my commands!"

Ancient and exhausted, the king wore this new burden with a tremendous weight. But in spite of his weariness, the king's eyes were still full of fire when he drew a deep breath to continue his edict.

"Prince Eino, Commander Agatha, and Commander Aaroni, I want you to assemble the knights and prepare them for battle immediately! We ride for the forest the moment your troops are ready. Don't delay. Their lives are in your hands."

"At once, my king," answered Prince Eino.

Commanders Agatha and Aaroni drew hunting horns from their backs. Eino drew his horn as well, though all three were tuned to different pitches, so that each commander could call their own troops. Walking out of the Throne Room, they retreated to the central courtyard. All the knights lived in the castle as well, so they could be called upon immediately in case of a crisis.

As the three commanders entered the courtyard, they looked up and noticed that the sky was turning a lighter blue. Dawn was about to break, and now they had to raise the alarm to thousands and thousands of knights who were sleeping peacefully in their quarters. Raising the horns to their lips, all three commanders sounded their calls at once, and all three clean, pure notes washed across the courtyard in a perfect triad, tuned so perfectly that no buzzing dissonances escaped as the bloom of sound brought every knight fully awake without hesitation.

Agatha and Aaroni didn't have to wait long while the knights dressed in their armor, mounted their horses, and assembled in the great courtyard. Before five minutes had passed, the last of the horses had blazed into the courtyard, bearing the entire army of Santara upon their backs.

The warriors were proud men whom had fought back many strange foes and fearlessly approached the courtyard, eager to meet with the fierce battle.

Their battle armor was polished magnificently, and turned them into dangerous forces, shining in the sun. The prince's men rode fully armed, sharp maces to one side and even deadlier war axes to the other, the blades jagged and triangular to sweep from both sides. Aaroni's knights carried longer axes that almost looked like scythes, and Agatha's troops all had excellent twin blades that swept to each side.

Eino, Agatha, and Aaroni watched the knights assemble, and as they were getting into their lines, their pages quickly brought the commanders' horses to their sides.

They rose into the saddles, and the horses all moved forward as soon as they landed, feeling the tension in their riders and only answering the pull of the reins a second later. Dressed in the best armor in the kingdom, Eino, Agatha, and Aaroni created a stunning picture before the army.

The commanders all wore the achievement of the country, a powerful lion rising out of the castle by the sea to protect it. In one arm, the lion brandished a sword. The ocean ran beneath the castle and shone blue on their armor.

On the shining armor of the knights and warriors, the other achievement of Santara stood proud. Three trefoils, each a symbol of the Trinity, stood proud above a wide shovel, a reminder that the people of Santara came from the dirt and worked the same dirt to make their survival from the rich lands.

Eino paused before he spoke, but only to steady his balance as the horse stirred beneath him, eager to sprint to battle.

"No time to waste! When we split up, follow your commander! Ride hard, knights!"

Eino turned his horse to face the wide promenade that opened into the outer courtyard, and the other commanders turned around as well.

As Prince Eino spurred his horse, the entire army rose to action, thousands of horses pouring across the courtyard and racing across the drawbridge as fast as they could get onto the bridge.

Ahead of them, the three commanders rode as fast as the wind, hoping that the knights would reach the villagers before it was too late.

When they got to the villages, the commanders could see hundreds still alive and fighting the monsters, but thousands more had already been slaughtered. The sight of the massacre was grotesque, but Eino and Agatha and Aaroni kept riding anyway. Their horses surged across the land from different directions to surprise the monsters.

The villagers used pikes and any other sharp weapons they had to hold back the monsters, standing their ground and not even hearing the horses behind them, being so caught up in terror of their foes.

Even as Agatha and Aaroni went off in different directions, splitting the army into three forces, Prince Eino saw the monsters surround one of the villagers, separating him from the others and tearing him limb from limb. Their walls of muscle covered in black fur made them seem almost shade-like as their night-dark fur absorbed the morning sun.

Hacking in both directions with the war-axes, the knights valiantly decapitated the monsters one by one, but as many as they could destroy the more came to rush after them.

The knights fought bravely, but the monsters had the upper hand in many regards. One knight rushed forward, swinging his war-axe, but the blade missed and only ripped the monster's abdomen. It swung viciously, and the horse screamed as torrents of blood poured from its forelegs. It fell over, dying from wounds to its chest, leaving the knight on the ground.

Other knights rushed to his side, while still others crowded through the villagers, turning them away from the battle and herding the survivors to safety.

The monster was still on its feet, even with the wound to its guts, thick ropes of strange matter holding its insides together. The knight screamed and swung his heavy mace, attempting the stun the monster, but the mace had no such effect on the great beast.

Agatha put up a valiant fight as she pummeled monster after monster with her great sword, tearing their limbs in her ferocity. She pushed toward the group of struggling knights, but too many monsters blocked her path. She watched as the monster felled two knights easily, gouging their necks before turning to the one still getting to his feet. With a tremendous roar, the monster moved forward and stopped just in front of the knight. The knight thought the pause would give him a chance, and he swung both his weapons at once, trying to crush the massive head.

The monster grabbed the knight's arms with its claws and smoothly ripped both arms away from the knight's body.

"Don't give up!" screamed Agatha. "Fight for your lives!"

Eino rushed toward a lone monster, and using his long sword, took several furious whacks. He was gratified when it stopped moving, but saw many more monsters threatening his knights. He raced back to the surge of battle, fighting his way through the monsters to reach the center of his forces, urging them forward and motivating them with his brilliant armor.

Once the villagers were herded away from the battlefield, they continued to run, led by the soldiers on their brave horses, ensuring that they were safe. A stray monster hunted them down, but was removed by the knights, who used their war-axes in tandem to swiftly bring it down. They resolutely hacked chunk after chunk out of its frame until the trauma became too great and it collapsed to the ground, proving no more of a threat as the villagers stampeded past its shaking body. The frantic villagers gave it space on the ground so they didn't get too close to its claws as they went through their last death-shakes.

The knights soon turned toward the deep hills, where many trees still grew, and inside these nestling hills, the villagers discovered a cave opening, almost too small to see and hidden by bushes and tall grass.

"Hide here, while these knights guard the entrance. When it's safe, we'll come get you."

As the massive rush of frightened villagers entered the cave, the rich forest hiding the entrance emptied, save for the two sentries still standing watch. Once the villagers were inside and organizing the bushes to hide the entrance as well as possible, he turned around on his horse and raced back to the battlefield.

As he rushed back out of the forest, he saw other knights fighting monsters as he went through the fields, but he was in too big of a hurry to lend his aid. He saw them fight valiantly, but as he got closer to the battle, he saw more and more of them falling beneath the massive claws of the monsters.

The roaring of the monsters as they died was a tremendous booming wave across the land. When the battle was the worst, the screaming of the knights became a shrill symphony pouring through the air. The two notes merged and created horrifying music as the two sides fought the brutal battle.

Red blood fled the knights' bodies and pooled on the ground, mixing with the black blood pouring from the many fallen monsters. It created an odious brown muck that spread across the battlefield until even the surviving soldiers were covered in the blending liquids as their metal boots splashed through.

When he reached the battlefield, he knew it was already a pitched battle. Although the line seemed strong, and the forces were holding their ground, just as many horses were leaving the fray, injured and unconscious riders on their backs.

He heard Prince Eino call, "Fall back! Fall back!"

The knight joined the rest of the escaping men, and pounded across the meadows, trying to make it to the castle with the rest of them.

But before he could get there, he heard a horrific roar behind him.

He kept riding, but as he fled, he felt a rushing pain across his neck.

Eino started counting the surviving knights and counted less than a couple thousand.

"Agatha! Aaroni! Go get the villagers! Get them to safety at the castle!"

Even in retreat, they had to continue hacking away at the monsters because they dogged their every step.

Although most of the surviving soldiers made it back to the castle, a few dozen were still slain as they ran. The closing doors held back the monsters none too soon, for as the survivors gathered in the courtyard, the knights dispersed to find the nurses, and the commanders headed for the Throne Room, the first deafening scrapes hit the door.

The claws of the monsters were sharp and tremendously long, but the doors were hewn from the largest timbers in the forest, and even the combined force of the monsters could not bring them down.

Far away in the cavern where the villagers hid, tension began to grow as the hours dragged on.

"I don't think they're coming back for us," said one of the farmers finally.

"They'd be here by now," agreed another.

The farmer went outside and got the sentry's attention. He entered the cave.

"We need you to find the other end of this cave. Can you do that for us?"

"Absolutely. Give me a fresh torch and some clay."

One of the potters produced a damp clump of white clay, perfect for marking the walls, while a farmer lit a fresh torch, the rags blazing to life at the first flicker of flint.

The sentry took the torch and the clay and headed off down the cave, treading carefully and marking the wall as he went.

Although a choice of turns confused him at first, the first choice he made brought him back to the cavern, so he turned the mark into an X and headed down the other passageway. Further through the dark cavern, he was faced with three exits, and he took the central one, marking it carefully. It was only a few hundred feet beyond that when he saw shadows forming on his torch. He put the torch behind him, looking forward.

As the guard's eyes adjusted, he was elated to see daylight. He made another mark in the wall, ran forward to confirm that the exit was in sight, and spied the lush forest beneath the volcano. The Bowmen had guarded this forest, and the Ravensblood River, for hundreds of years. The villagers would be safe here.

Turning around, the guard followed his marks back through the caverns, happy to see the villagers undiscovered inside. He eagerly led them through, and when they saw the forest and the eager Bowmen coming forward to meet them, they relaxed and were very happy.

The Bowmen erected enough tents for everyone and soon they were settled.

Settled in this new forest, the villagers now had to wait for news from the castle on what was to come.

The leader of the Bowmen spoke to the villagers. "All of you can take refuge here. Our home is your home. You can stay as long as you want. We have plenty of fish in the Ravensblood River. We never go hungry here."

"Thank you so much for your protection," answered one of the farmers.

"We're happy to protect you."

Chapter Four

The Knights and the Castle

General Eino, Aaroni, Agatha, and the sentry all approached the inner chamber where King Aro waited.

King Aro's throne room was lit with hundreds of candles in massive candelabras. Almost no one was inside the Throne Room. Only King Aro, ten of his closest advisors, and his servant, Sarah, a woman in rags.

As Eino, Agatha, and Aaroni advanced, all eyes focused on them. The sentry walked ahead of them.

Eino addressed the king after bowing humbly. "King Aro, there's too many of them! Thousands of our soldiers are dead. We have no choice. I think we're going to have to call on the book of protection."

King Aro nodded his head sagely. "These gates are holding now, but they won't hold for long. But I sense an even deeper darkness this time. Something is different."

Eino nodded his head. "This is something way beyond our power. We truly need the power of the Goddess of Light."

Sarah was busy cleaning the blood off the armor of the soldiers assembled in the Throne Room when she heard a dark, menacing whisper in her ear. It was so disturbing she had to stop rubbing the blood away and take a step back, listening with growing horror.

The voice whispered, "You deserve so much better than this, more than being just a common servant. Go to the king. Offer him much comfort. He'll see your true worth. Go."

Sarah walked over to the king. As she crossed the Throne Room, she heard him talking, and she noticed Prince Eino standing near. She heard Eino say,

"Yes, my king, I think the White Book of Summonings is our best hope."

Sarah nodded and spoke to Eino, addressing him humbly. "How wise you are, dear prince."

King Aro turned to his trusty servant. "Sarah!"

"Yes, my king?"

King Aro looked her directly in the eyes. "In the Great Library," and at this Sarah flinched in fear, "behind the double doors, you will find the White Book of Summonings. Bring it back here to me at once!"

Sarah bowed. "Right away, my king," she answered. She moved quickly out of the room to the back corridor where the black stone spiral stairs led down to the bottom levels of the castle, and also, far below, the Great Library of Santara's darkest magic and most ancient histories.

Sarah pushed opened the large double doors and entered the library. The only sounds were the crackling from scattered candle flames, the whispering of hushed voices, and the small scratches of quills on paper as new magic was recorded. Sarah could see the two double doors at the other end of the long library. The huge stone pillars supporting the stone ceiling separated the bookcases. Magnificent tapestries hung on the ends of the cedar shelves identified the different subjects—Herbalism, History of the Kingdom, Spells, Curses, and Healing Potions. The closer Sarah got to the doors, the slower she walked. She was very afraid of what was behind them.

Without warning, the doors to the secret chamber burst open with so much force that the wind knocked Sarah over. She fell, crying out, to the stone floor. She was stunned for a few seconds.

The cold from the floor seeped into her bones. She realized she had to get up. As she pushed herself off the floor, she stumbled as she got to her feet. Although she couldn't see anyone in the room, she could hear an evil voice whispering in her head.

"You shall never remember what's happening here."

Sarah looked around, confused. She could see inside the chamber, with the two books inside, but she felt like she wasn't in control. She felt like she was in some kind of trance.

As Sarah struggled, trying to break free, she felt her body being pushed, persuaded, into the chamber. She followed, although every step filled her with dread and made her want to retreat.

Deep inside the secret chamber, two special books were kept. These were the most powerful books of magic in the whole kingdom. Sarah stared at the precious volumes in fascination.

The black book was locked in a chest long ago, and true to the stories, an oak chest hunkered in the corner. Labeled *The Dark Book of Summonings*, it was a twisted volume with dark red letters on the front, and claws on the edges of the book showed its dark nature. Sarah heeded the rumors and ignored the box as best she could.

This book sat peacefully, with gold lettering on its cover, as well as flowers around the words, inside a glass frame, protected and pristine. The glass frame was encased in a slab of stone, which bore down on the stone table and protected the book from any invaders.

Suddenly, Sarah heard a low growling sound in the air, as if magic was being summoned from a distant realm.

An evil, dark blue mist slowly began to form over the book and she watched the mist grow thicker as it surrounded the tome.

The growling was much louder by this point, and as it reached a fever pitch, the white book lifted off the stone case and levitated into the middle of the glassed chamber.

As the mist grew denser, the cover of the book began to twist and swirl. The flowers lifted off the surface. Everything was hung in midair. Then there was a big puff of black smoke rushing out of the blue cloud. As it covered the books, the illusion had been cast.

The Dark Book of Summonings had now been completely disguised as the white book.

Sarah stood there spellbound, not sure what to do, even though she had seen the events transpire with her own eyes. She turned her head back and forth between the two books, confused.

"Are your eyes deceiving you? Have you lost your vision? Grab the white book and be gone from this place!"

Sarah knew instinctively that the voice in her head was dangerous, and the sickening feeling of falling sent her stomach into a tailspin, but she was still caught in the trance, and the ropes of control pulled her back from the brink of collapse and panic, pulling her into line and persuading her to pick up the white book.

Sarah tried to fight the trance, but she had lost her power. As her hand reached out for the book, she tried to close her eyes so she wouldn't have to see. But even as she shut her eyes, the book touched her hand, and suddenly, all the pressure was gone from her mind.

Sarah looked around the chamber, breathing heavily, trying to get her bearings. She recalled the instructions that King Aro had told her, so she headed for the exit of the chamber, glad to leave the library and return to her king, who was far more powerful than she was.

As Sarah walked back out of the chamber, closing the doors behind her, she heard an evil laugh. She turned around and shuddered, glad to be rid of that dark force in her mind.

Her hands shook violently as she clutched the book against her chest. As she walked up the spiral staircase, she began to feel drained from the long climb, and she leaned against the railing for support.

She gasped for breath, but after a few seconds of leaning there, her strength returned, and she finished her ascent without thinking twice about it.

Chapter Five

The Curse is Cast

Prince Eino listened carefully. Since King Aro had begun his plan, the silence outside had been complete. No monsters scraped the doors or thumped against the walls with their shoulders, and now only silence reigned outside.

At that moment, Sarah arrived back in the throne room with the book.

"Give me that book!" said the king.

Sarah's hands were gripped so tight she couldn't let go.

King Aro took the book forcefully out of Sarah's hands and slammed it on the table before him. But before King Aro could complete the ritual, he needed to make himself humble. He removed his crown and placed it on the table. Then his also removed his battle-gloves, his rings, his other jewelry, his cloak, and his bracelets. Once he had been humbled, only then did the king begin to speak to the Goddess in humble prayer.

"Oh Goddess of Light, hear my plea! I am your humble servant. My kingdom is under attack by vicious, wild beasts. Render your aid! Please, Goddess of Light, answer my humble prayer." Then he began to pray in the old Latin tongue to invoke the Goddess herself. *"Attende Domina, et miserere quia peccavimus tibi."* In the modern world, the translation would be, "Hear us, O Goddess, and have mercy, for we have sinned against you." General Eino understood the words to mean something else.

As he repeated the prayer over and over again, the stone floor quietly began to rumble, growing stronger by the second. Above the middle of the throne room, the air thickened and churned with energy. Thick wisps of blue smoke began wafting and swirling until combustion brought flames floating through the air in the middle of the Throne Room. The advisors, the servant, the king, and all the knights stared in awe at the magic door that was being created from some other world.

Through this portal stepped the most beautiful woman. Ice blue satin shimmered around her body as if it was dancing across her skin. Jewels and fine lace encrusted the edges, unburned by the strange blue flames in the air. The skin of her face was pale, but her lips were bright and moist.

For all appearances, she was the Goddess of Light. Everyone stared at her in awe and worship.

However, as the Goddess looked at Eino, her eyes flashed a strange red color, and in an instant, Prince Eino knew for sure that this woman was not who she appeared to be.

Prince Eino felt his pulse slow down as the shock hit him full force. Instead of summoning the Goddess of Light, King Aro had accidentally summoned the red-eyed Evil Sorceress, glamourized to look like the Goddess of Light.

He stepped back in shock, and clutched his chest as his heart began to race, responding to the shock by pumping harder, forcing him to stay on his feet.

Prince Eino cried out a warning, trying to turn the tide he had unknowingly unleashed. "King Aro, something's wrong! That isn't the Goddess of Light!"

The woman floating through the air looked down at Prince Eino. With a harsh, menacing voice, she declared, "That's right, Prince Eino! I'm not the Goddess of Light!"

The beautiful silk skin vanished, covered by dark, leathery surfaces. This was hardly skin, but weather-beaten hide. Her once beautiful white hair turned dark and menacing, flowing past her feet down to the floor, where it slithered and troubled the subjects. Her shining body now loomed down as the Evil Sorceress brandished her true form.

"Curse the goddesses that bless you, for they turned their backs on me!" she screamed.

Meanwhile, King Aro had taken the moment to escape, heading to his chambers, where he kept a special spear to fight things of evil. The Goddess of Light had blessed it herself, centuries ago, and it had never failed him.

The woman disguised as the Goddess began to utter an evil spell. "Animalia Transformalia!" She continued speaking in a strange language. As she spoke, her eyes flared bright red and continued to shine, wide open and furious. "Anamalia Transformalia!"

All the soldiers began to turn toward the exits, but even as they started to move, the great doors slammed tightly shut of their own free will. Only a second later did they hear the Evil Sorceress sucking the air away from the room, forcing the doors shut with her violent intent.

Trapped inside the Throne Room, hundreds of soldiers turned toward the Evil Sorceress, determined to stop her. But even as they ran toward her, the spell began to take effect, and they slowed down, trying to take stock of their bodies.

Feeling sick to their stomachs, the knights paused, waiting for what would happen next.

Prince Eino felt very strange, as if his bones were being stretched. He could tell from the scattered screams that the soldiers were being transformed too.

The screams built higher around him until even Prince Eino himself began to scream.

The Evil Sorceress laughed darkly. "During the day you are humans, by night you are lions. Now you are Lion-People. You are banished to the Forbidden Forest, where no one will ever look on your faces again."

As the three soldiers turned into lions, they began to scream. Prince Eino felt like his bones were being ripped through his skin. He could see new muscles bulging and stretching under his arms, and it felt like they were on fire. As he lost touch with his humanity, he let out a gigantic roar. Whiskers began to grow on his chin.

Eino saw the woman knight, Agatha, also screaming in pain. Suddenly, one last glimpse of his humanity returned. Although he had almost been turned into a lion, he was able to force himself to speak hoarsely.

Prince Eino watched all the lions appearing before him. As they completely turned, Prince Eino noticed that their coats were breathtaking, almost gilded, vibrant shining hair. He was proud of his new frame and felt no bond with the evil creature that had transmuted him. He roared in heavy defiance, and the roar echoed through the Throne Room, inciting the other lions, which quickly joined him in the vicious call.

The Evil Sorceress was furious, and her eyes flashed even brighter.

As she remained distracted by the curse, she did not see King Aro ascend the staircase behind her. He shoved the spear forward with all his remaining strength, embedding it in her back. She screamed hideously, and a blue vapor spread out from the ring of flames. With a piercing scream emerging from her shocked throat, the ring of flames consumed her in a single sucking whirlpool and the circle spun firmly shut with a loud bang.

But by this time, Eino, Agatha, and Aaroni, and all the other knights in the Throne Room were all lions. They turned away and ran as fast as they could towards the forest.

As the lions ran away, Queen Agnes looked out the window and cried, "The black monsters are gone!" Her cries floated down the balconies, and the sentries outside the Throne Room picked up the cry. King Aro heard the cry as well.

All the knights could do was roar at each other as they scrambled towards the safety of the dark woods. Over time, as day after day allowed them their humanity, they slowly began to build a life and have descendants. Deep inside the Forbidden Forest, they found a new way to live.

King Aro watched the lions disappear into the distance. He paced back and forth, furious about what had happened and what almost happened.

"Eino was right about the book. She deceived even me! From now on I declare the library to be locked and sealed forever! No one should ever take the chance of releasing her again!"

The Goddess of Light finally emerged after the danger was past. "She's gone now. I had the strength to trap her where she can't escape again."

"Good," said King Aro. "I hope she never bothers Santara again. Can you break the curse from Prince Eino and the others?"

The Goddess of Light hung her head. "I'm sorry, King Aro, but I'm too weak. The Evil Sorceress drained my powers. But fear not, she wasn't able to turn them into the evil monsters. I stopped her from doing that to your knights."

Chapter Six

The Princess

Two hundred years later, the same two moons still shone down upon Santara. The sun still shone brightly and the birds still sang. For two hundred years, the people had not been troubled by evil. But inside the castle, trouble was brewing.

The tall spires of the castle reached hundreds of feet into the sky. Flags with white swans on a blue background above a purple ocean marked the royal colors. Beneath one of the taller spires was where Princess Alzena lived. She was arguing with her nanny, Margaret.

Her nanny cried, "Sit still! Sit still, I said!"

"Stop bossing me around!" shouted Princess Alzena.

"Sit still then!"

The palace nanny wore a plain black dress with a few white highlights, still just another servant of the king. As she had aged in life, had become chubby, but she was still feisty. White streaks were beginning to tease into her black hair, tied up in a painful bun, and her cheeks were on the edge of being rosy. She had narrow eyes that sneered at people disdainfully and the corners were wrinkled from many years of hard work.

Alzena was 22, and only had a red corset on, still halfway laced up. Her long red hair flowed down to the floor gracefully. Her sea-blue eyes pouted back at her from the mirror. She sat defensively in the chair, with her arms crossed, and continued arguing.

"But you know I want to go get my cloudberries. They are my favorite!"

Margaret answered with a frustrated grimace and a grunt. Taking a deep breath to calm herself, she patiently explained, "But you need to get your clothes on, Alzena. Those nice suitors are downstairs, waiting for your arrival. You have responsibilities."

Alzena angrily brushed her long red hair, although she still glowered into the mirror and continued to argue even as she was getting ready.

"But why can't I enjoy the things I used to?" asked Alzena. "Why is everything always about responsibilities?"

Margaret sighed. "Because you are the princess!"

Alzena's expression softened as she remembered her grandmother. She stood up and looked out the window off into the distance, remembering a happier time.

"I remember when my grandmother used to lead me by the hand to marketplace and we'd get fresh cloudberries. She would take me back home and make the most delicious cloudberry jam. When I used to put it on the biscuits with hot butter, it was the best taste in the world. I miss those days."

Margaret, seeing her distracted, started lacing up the corset again. "You have to get rid of those childish notions," said Margaret. "You're an adult now, you have responsibilities—you need to get married. You need to carry on the royal line."

"What are you doing?" said Alzena, suddenly noticing the tightening of the corset. She swatted Margaret's hands away, and Margaret backed up in alarm, none too soon because Alzena stood up and turned around, seething in rage and clenching her fists at her sides until they turned white with tension. "Stop that at once! Didn't you hear me? Leave me now!" commanded Alzena.

Margaret, knowing her place, bowed and left the room.

After the door had closed completely, Alzena waited a couple more seconds, then looked at her reflection and pumped her arms triumphantly. As she did so, she realized that the corset was still constricting her. She frantically pulled it off and threw it onto the bed, screaming, "I've always hated these blasted corsets!"

Alzena looked around the room, and knelt down and dragged a long yellow dress out from under the bed. She quickly donned the peasant robes, and her plain tan hood covered her dark red hair so she was completely indistinguishable from a commoner.

She snuck out of her bedroom and walked down a long stone hallway. Down the stairs she could see a very ungainly prince that she knew was going to be her suitor and walked briskly past, disguised so well he didn't even notice her. She also saw other well-dressed men milling about, obviously waiting for her grand entrance. She swept past them, undetected. As she left down another corridor, she whispered under her breath, "None of them are suitable for me." But of course they were all talking to each other and didn't notice.

As she headed down the hallway, she heard the banging of pots and pans and the yelling of the palace cooks as they struggled to make all the meals on time. As she walked in, someone dropped a large dish of food, and everyone laughed in unison at him. Only the head cook saw her. He'd been getting good vegetables and fruits from Alzena's excursions in the marketplace for many years, and he didn't mind helping her escape.

"Don't forget to get me some of those cloudberries too!" he shouted this time. Alzena waved as she left, her sign that she would.

From the wide cobblestone pathway winding down the hill, Alzena could smell the delicious food being cooked in the marketplace, and she could hear the distant shouts of hucksters and musicians, a wonderful, bustling oasis far different from the disapproving glares and boring endless stones of the palace walls. Alzena walked down the street, undetected, away from the palace.

A short time later, Margaret rushed into the kitchen, looking left and right with her beady eyes at the cooks.

"Did you see a woman walking through here, a woman that might have been the princess?" she asked.

"With all the meals I have to cook," exploded the head chef, "how do you think I have time to keep track of everyone that comes running in and out of here all the time? Besides, what are you doing here anyway? You're just a common servant. We're all busy down here!"

"Fine then," she said. "Don't help me! I'll just be on my way."

Flustered, she bustled out of the kitchen and back through the castle. She was headed to talk to the king about her problems dealing with Alzena and she was in a very bad mood. As she got closer to the suitors, one called out, "Hey, have you seen Alzena?"

"She shooed me out of the room, but the last time I saw her, she was getting dressed." She smiled. "I'm sure it won't be long now."

Then, as she turned away, her smile disappeared and was replaced by her normal flustered demeanor.

Chapter Seven

The Noble King Pajari

King Pajari was almost forty-nine, but he looked much older because of all his diplomatic responsibilities as king. The skin under his eyes was baggy and puffy from lack of sleep, and even though his beard was braided and festooned with ribbons, there was no gladness in his eyes— deep hazel eyes with huge bushy eyebrows resting above in a glare.

It was only royal tradition that the beard be finely decorated that made him keep allowing it. Strong muscles from the years spent fighting had been overlaid by years of diplomacy and extra weight. Although two lovely servants took care of his every need, he still lay in bed and watched the ceiling. His red hair was turning gray now. His royal bedclothes were silk pants embroidered with white swans, and his shirt was in the colors of the kingdom—blue, white and purple.

As he rested in bed, he heard a persistent knock on the door, and then the annoying voice of Margaret.

Margaret cried out through the door, "King Pajari Aro, I must speak with you!"

Surprised and annoyed, he took a deep breath and sat up in bed, stretching his arms and looking at the servants. Recognizing the signal, they both got up without a word and picked up a magnificent deep red velvet robe of power, gold-trimmed, reserved for the king. Holding one arm each, they carried it over to him and, with practiced skill, slipped it over his arms, and donned the royal crown. Only then did he stand up and nod to the door.

The servants walked over and opened it.

Standing there in all his glory, King Pajari glared at Margaret and said, "What is it now?"

The palace nanny wrung her hands. "Oh, King Pajari, it's terrible. Princess Alzena has run off to the marketplace again. Prince Yuli and the other suitors are still waiting for her down by the courtyard. It's a complete disaster!"

King Pajari started to pace back and forth with his hands folded behind his back, fuming and glowering.

"This is the fourth suitor she's stood up like this. Really, I just can't take anymore! How many royal suitors do I have to write? There are only so many kingdoms in these lands! I just can't condone her behavior anymore!"

Exasperated, King Pajari turned his face away from the door and Margaret and threw a long, brooding look out the window as if he could burn holes through people just by staring at them.

Queen Lydia walked in behind him, quietly, to avoid being noticed. The queen was already dressed in her royal finery and had more energy, being ten years younger than the king. Her blue eyes shone, and her strawberry blonde hair flowed in intricate braids down her back. She was caught up in some business around the castle, but could hear the shouting clearly through the door and came in to see what all the trouble was about. After all, a good castle could never survive without a good queen at the helm.

King Pajari was still glaring out the window, thinking. Finally, he snapped, "She's exactly like her mother!"

At that Queen Lydia spoke up. "Did you just mention me, my king?"

The king didn't answer right away, just kept glowering. He knew he was going to have to talk to her now. He didn't want the servants to hear what he had to say. He turned around, looking only at the servants waiting for his command.

"Leave us!" he said in a deep commanding voice, and the servants left the room without saying a word, terrified into submission by his threatening presence. The queen continued to watch him, unflustered by his vanity and thunder. She still saw the vulnerable man deep inside.

King Pajari looked at the queen finally. "It's your daughter—she took off again!"

The queen breathed out sharply. Her shoulders rose with tension. She sat down on the bed to compose herself.

"You know, dear husband, she just has not been the same since your sweet mother, may the Goddess of Light bless her soul, passed away. You know how close they were to each other. "

King Pajari lowered his head in acknowledgement and prayer, conceding the point. Queen Lydia continued to negotiate, sensing her strength. She added, "And you know you hold on to her too tightly. What harm could there be in the princess spending time with the common people—her people?"

The king slammed his fist down in anger on the table. Queen Lydia stiffened with surprise.

"Because she's the princess!" he roared. "The only princess in the castle. I don't have any princes to carry on the line. She is the future of this kingdom. She's all I have and I can't take the risk of losing her! She has responsibilities!" He noticed that Queen Lydia was still stiff and he lowered his voice and pleaded. "She's all I have."

Knowing he was right and feeling ashamed, the queen lowered her head. "I'm sorry I offended you, my king. I'm sorry I couldn't give you any boys. The Goddess took them away from me. All I could give you was Alzena."

King Pajari's hand clenched into a fist. "Together, we have to bring an end to this rebellious nature of hers. If she was ever hurt—" He let the threat trail off, thinking otherwise.

Queen Lydia stood and turned to go. "All right," she said, "I'll talk to Alzena. The Goddess of Light knows I've always understood her better than you."

She opened the door and left. The king saw a palace guard standing outside the door, and while the door was open, he motioned to him to come in. The guard came in the room, undetected by the queen, and closed the door quietly behind him.

"Yes, your Majesty?" asked the guard.

King Pajari quietly said, "Bruno, I want you to be on the lookout for my daughter. She is on the loose again. Don't let everyone know what's going on, just Dax. I don't trust the rest of these guards. Just ask about her bright red hair. If you find her, bring her to me."

"Yes, my king," answered the guard. Then he left, closing the door behind him again, and headed off to find Alzena.

After the guard left, King Pajari went on his own way through the castle to find the suitors. He did not see the shadow from behind him, a small wisp of smoke in the air. As he was going down the hallway, he heard a soft, tantalizing female voice whispering in his ear, although he could see nothing out of the ordinary.

"The prince you are looking for is Yuli. All the other ones you can send home. But Yuli has what it takes to be the prince of this kingdom."

King Pajari looked around as the voice faded away, but he couldn't see anything wrong with her argument. Satisfied that he was well informed, he walked into the chamber where three suitors, dressed up in finery and talking, stood in the hallway drinking his wine and eating his food.

"Which one of you suitors is Prince Yuli from Sunray Island?"

"I am," piped up one of the suitors.

"You should stay here with me. You would be a great match for my daughter. The rest of you, go home. If I have need of you again, you will be notified."

Prince Yuli and the king walked down the hallway together, chatting. As they did so, a dark shadow formed behind them. There was the briefest shudder of laughter, and then the shadow faded away.

Chapter Eight

The Forbidden Forest

The Forbidden Forest was a dark and dangerous place. Ignored by the citizens of Santara for two hundred years, it had provided a wonderful place for the Lion-People to live and flourish. Even on that fateful day when Alzena ran away from the palace, the forest was still inhabited by animals, butterflies, and lizards that ran through the untouched forest as if it was their own.

However, this was also the domain of the Lion-People. After being exiled to the forest, they had begun to make a clearing deep in the woods where the trees were cut down around a sacred spring that flowed all year round. The Lion-People tended carefully to the spring, never harming the ground near it that gave them life-giving water. The forest around the village was left untouched, and grasses and herbs grew on the roofs of the cabins. The cabins were made out of wood and stones, for they had nothing else in the forest to build with.

For two hundred years the community had survived there, complete with every necessity. Far away from the village was the sanctuary, a place of deep reverence where Eino, Agatha, and Aaroni stood, preserved as lions by the mystery of the place for hundreds of years, still dressed in the armor of the kingdom, quietly watching.

The burial place was deep underground, with great stones holding up the roof of the cave. The air seemed thinner inside the deep cave.

Cato was standing in front of his grandfather's resting place that day because it was the day of remembrance. On the day of remembrance, everyone in the village had to visit the resting place of their ancestors. Other Lion-People stood in the cavern visiting the places, leaving flowers on the markers, and speaking and praying to their ancestors.

As Cato stared at the resting place of his grandfather, he prayed as well. "Dear Grandfather, I want to travel beyond the forest. I know it's been done before. I know it's dangerous, but I can't live with myself unless I go. I need your blessing, please, Grandfather."

As Cato kneeled there, he felt a surge of energy go through his legs. He stood up in shock and looked around himself. Although he was used to the nightly transformation, the whiskers on his face were beginning to stretch out. As he looked around, he saw the other people, very deeply in touch with their lion side, others spontaneously transforming from the magic energy of the place.

Cato breathed deeply and peacefully, and he felt his whiskers retract again. Even though the moment of energy and fluctuation was gone, every hair on his body was standing on end. He saw a woman nearby. She was transforming more, getting very much in touch with her ancestors.

The feeling that his grandfather had touched him would not go away. Cato felt he had the sign he was looking for. He strode with purpose back to his village, back to the house he shared with his mother, and left the cave and the sanctuary behind.

All the Lion-People looked subtly like lions, even in the daytime when the curse allowed them to be human. They had long flowing hair, thick mustaches and beards, and small noses with thin lips, and they also lived with an animal's reverence of nature.

Cato's house was on the outskirts of the village, although all the houses were connected by small stone walkways, as well as wooden hand-railings, and everything was built around the spring in the center of town. Water flowed freely from this spring, and many creeks began there. Along the stones of the lanes one would find flowing streams of clear water, and many birds flew happily through the air.

Inside the house, it was also as cozy as they could make it. Cato was a wood-carver by nature, and he excelled at creating animals from pieces of wood. These were not just animal figures, though. Cato was able to carve these wooden animals into chairs, tables, pipes, and many other things. His skills were prized in the village.

But when he told his mother that he was going to leave, it seemed like all the brightness left the room, and deep furrows formed across Lena's brow, and her piercing green eyes glared at him. She frowned fitfully and stared up at Cato, who was taller than her by nearly a foot.

Lena stomped the floor of the cabin.

"I've told you hundreds of times you can't leave the Forbidden Forest!"

Cato growled back at her, filled with passion. "But how do you know the legends are true, Mother?" asked Cato.

Lena tried not to cry when she heard that. She twisted her face and swallowed hard, but Cato was not blind to his mother's pain. He was just too mad to care.

Lena responded, "Because—you don't understand, I saw one of the Lion-People leave, and he never came back. I could lose you forever!"

Cato stood up in defiance, tired of hearing the old arguments. As he grabbed his pack—the one carrying everything he would need—with an angry flourish, he gave his mother the answer that was in his heart.

"Well, Mother, I know how they felt! I have to see what's out there! I have to take that chance!"

He stormed to the door and pushed it open with more force than necessary. As he stormed away from the house into the forest, he could hear Lena calling behind him desperately as he left.

"Cato! Cato, please! Come back! Listen to reason."

But Lena's cries faded into the distance as Cato went into the forest away from the village, and soon nothing but silence and trees surrounded Cato.

All around him was dark green grass, towering ferns, lizards, and butterflies. There was no path, for few ever left the Forbidden Forest, but Cato was a hunter through his lion's strength and he knew the way to the edge of the forest. A brook rushed wildly near him, over rocks and through logs, and the sound was like raindrops against the rocks.

Up ahead the trees grew even thicker, but he could still see the sun high above through breaks in the canopy, and he knew he was heading the right way. The trees seemed to form a tunnel before him, and moss covered every surface in a living green carpet. His leather boots were crisscrossed with leather laces—from a deer he had killed many years ago—all the way up to his knees. But even as high as his boots were, his legs were soaked with moisture from the ferns and grasses as he moved through the forest, searching for the edge and the mysterious curse that kept them held inside.

However, there finally came a place where the trees were thinner, and up ahead, he could see light shining through the endless river of branches surrounding him since the day he was born. The sight made his heart beat quicker and his feet move faster. It seemed to take forever for him to escape the forest. The light grew brighter and brighter through the trees, and the undergrowth made way for bushes and even clear spaces. He was running so fast by the time he broke through the trees and out into the open meadow that, for a second, he forgot about the curse and just leapt out of the trees, trying to stop himself as he remembered the force that should have stopped him.

He landed on the ground and stood still, and looked all over his body. He was not turning to stone, as the stories said. Nor did he catch fire and burn as others had told him. In fact, nothing bad happened at all. He was so overjoyed that he was right that nothing could hide his pleasure anymore. He let out a long, victorious roar.

Cato stared at the brilliant sun shining down on him, and then, blinking from the brightness, looked out across golden, sun-washed meadows full of wheat and corn, and even further the magnificent world of Santara, which included towering mountains, a distant castle, and a dark blue expanse that puzzled Cato.

Curious to see this strange new world he was finally able to explore, Cato made his way across the meadow towards where the stone roads began to stretch. There was a long distance between him and places where the people had cultivated the land. Their fear of the Forbidden Forest was so great that they had left a wide swath of land untended. After he crossed that, he found himself on a road beside a river.

Chapter Nine

The Fisherman

Cato was headed in the direction of the castle and the marketplace. A broad river flowed near him, and he stopped for a drink of clear water.

Suddenly, he heard a voice call out, "Wait! Don't run!"

Cato stopped where he was kneeling. A fisherman stood nearby.

"Excuse me," said Cato. "I will just be on my way."

"I know who you are, Cato. Please stay where you are," said the fisherman.

Cato wrinkled his brows in confusion. "How do you know my name?" he asked.

"Well, don't you recognize me, Cato?" He smiled, and as Cato stared at him, his eyes opened wide in recognition.

"It that you, Kainuu? Your great grandmother was one of the Three—Agatha! How is this possible? No one's seen you for ten years. Your mother still mourns you."

Kainuu smiled at being recognized. "I've been living here, outside of the Forbidden Forest, and plying my trade as a fisherman. But this definitely was not the life you were expecting. No good will ever come of you leaving the Forbidden Forest. If I were you, I would go straight back where you came from."

Cato shook himself and stared straight back. "No," he said, shaking his head. "I can't let my fears rule me anymore. I made it out of the Forbidden Forest without being hurt, and now I know you've been alive for the last ten years. Now I have to know what's in this world."

Kainuu smiled at him. "I appreciate your courage. But then at least let me prepare you for the world. You could never enter the marketplace with your hair making you look like a lion all day long. Come inside so we can talk."

Kainuu motioned to a hut nearby, surrounded by lures and traps. Cato followed him inside.

The inside of Kainuu's hut was just like the outside, crammed with lures and lobster pots. In the corner, a fireplace crackled, keeping the entire shack nice and warm. Kainuu started boiling tea in a kettle he hung above the fireplace.

"Please, Cato," said Kainuu, "take a seat over there."

Cato sat down in a chair by the fireplace.

Kainuu kept his fingers laced and his head low as he told his tale. "When I walked out of the Forbidden Forest ten years ago, I was a couple of years younger than you are now. I was so brave and full of wonder. I didn't care what they said. I wanted to explore the world outside the cage of that forest."

Cato smiled in agreement. He spoke up. "That's what the forest has always felt like to me as well. A cage. You must be so happy and free here."

Kainuu looked up at Cato. "Oh, if only the world was so simple, Cato! I didn't fit in here either. I have to live on the edge of civilization, becoming a fisherman and a loner, hiding every night like a criminal! The people here in Santara, they have ridiculed me because of my looks. They say I look too much like a lion. The guards wanted to arrest me because they simply suspect me of being one of the Lion-People and I had no choice but to flee here!"

Cato looked in surprise towards Kainuu. "Surely, if they knew who you were, what you were capable of, they wouldn't treat you like that."

"But Cato, they still believe the old stories told about us, the stories they were telling two hundred years ago. They don't see us as people. They see us as monsters. They are a scared and superstitious people. I have to hide every night when I change. I can't ever risk being seen at night."

"I thought that as soon as we stepped out of the Forbidden Forest, the curse was lifted!" said Cato.

Kainuu shook his head. "No, Cato. It will never end for us. There's no way to ever break this curse."

As Cato and Kainuu were talking, the tea began to boil with a loud popping and sizzling as drops of water began to hit the flames. Kainuu walked over to the fire, got the tea kettle, and poured the tea into two clay teacups.

When Kainuu sat back down, he continued. "Cato, please listen. I know you want to explore your newfound freedom, this great new world, but I'm just as trapped here as I was in the forest. What if they kill you?" he whispered. "With your long whiskers and beard, you'd be recognized as one of the Lion-People right away. And your hair looks like it hasn't been cut since the day you were born. You can't visit the marketplace looking uncivilized. One of the things I learned from these people was how to cut hair properly. A few minutes in the chair with my tools, and you'll look like you were born in the marketplace, not the forest."

Kainuu pushed his chair out to stand and walked over to Cato. Cato stood up in protest, protecting his beard with his hands. "But this hair is sacred!" said Cato.

"I know this is hard for you. But you wanted to explore the great big world and this is what you have to do first."

"Okay, I'll do it," said Cato. He sat down nervously in the chair as Kainuu grabbed a pair of scissors. Cato had never seen these metal blades before, and he stiffened. "Relax, it's for your hair," Kainuu reassured him.

As Cato's red-brown locks fell to the floor behind him, he felt as if the power of the forest was falling away from him, his heritage falling away in clumps. As Kainuu came around to the front, Cato held his hand over his beard and said, "Wait. I need to say goodbye to it first." He paused for a few seconds, closing his eyes. "Okay," he said. "Now I'm ready. Take my beard off."

As the last of his hair fell away, Cato felt as though the forest was lost to him forever. He had begun a new life, and these were the first steps. Kainuu brought out some clothes covered in fine embroidery and blocked with deep blue muslin.

"Here," said Kainuu, "come outside, and look at the man you are now!"

Cato followed Kainuu out to the river. In its clear, still reflection where the water calmed by the banks, he could see a whole new person staring back at him. All of his beautiful hair had been replaced by a sharp jawline, rugged cheeks, and going up to his temples he only saw faint vestiges of the sideburns that used to be there. The clothes were nothing like the skins he had to wear in the forest where they had nothing to live off of but what they could find. He looked very much like Kainuu now.

"Please remember, Cato, wherever you go, you have to get back here by sunset, so you are well hidden when you change at night. If they see you change, they will hunt you down for fear and take your life."

"Relax, Kainuu. Everything will be fine. I will be back before sundown. I feel like I will be able to handle myself now, thanks to your help."

Kainuu put his hands on Cato's shoulders and patted them reassuringly.

"There now," he said, "you're all ready for the big world. Go forth, and may the Goddess of Light be with you."

Cato walked on down the road towards the marketplace, feeling much better than before.

Chapter Ten

The Marketplace

The magnificent Castle Aro, where Alzena escaped not too long ago, sat imposingly over the marketplace, casting a grey shadow down off the hills into the marketplace below, as if trying to assert its power over the common people.

The bustling marketplace had huge walls around it made of very heavy stones, and a massive gate with many flags on it marked the entrance to the marketplace. The huge gate was closed every night to protect the people from the fearsome beasts they still believed prowled the countryside.

Inside the marketplace gates finally, Cato could see many tents, each one brighter than the next. Brilliant colors on every one threatened to outdo one another as they vied for attention from the passing shoppers. This was a place where everybody came to mingle, from the guards to the common peasants to the merchants, a place where everyone was welcome.

One vendor called out from his booth, "Fish pies! Hot fish pies!" Cato had no doubt it was made with fish from Kainuu's catch. Another vendor was crying out further down the way, "Cloudberries! Fresh cloudberries!"

Cato approached the rows of vendors with caution. Even though he was dressed correctly, he didn't want to say anything out of place that might attract attention to his nature. Behind him he heard another vendor shout, "Juicy pickles! Fresh juicy pickles!" Having nothing to trade or make any payment with, Cato tried to stay out of the way of the crowd.

Music from flutes and harps and lutes all playing together in a street band came pouring out of the market, music that made some people dance around him. As he listened, he was fascinated because in the Forbidden Forest there were never any instruments to make music.

As he was listening, he noticed two young children running down the way. The first child was dressed as a lion, with scraps of wool attached to burlap for a mane and a piece of string flopping around for a tail.

The child running behind him had a piece of wood for a sword and a mud-covered bag trying to look like a suit of armor because the mud was gray but falling off the bag.

The lion boy was yelling, "Rraarr!"

The other boy dressed as a knight was yelling, "Yah! Yah!"

The knight ran after the lion-boy. Cato was even happier that he was out of the way of all the foot traffic.

It was at this moment that Princess Alzena entered the marketplace from the other side leading up to the castle, looking around for fresh cloudberries among other things. She got a few apples and lemons, but finally found the berries.

As she got the cloudberries, Cato noticed her. Although she was disguised, Cato still saw that she was a beautiful woman, and even though the other people seemed to be ignoring her, Cato was fixated by her presence. He stopped paying attention to the marketplace around him.

Alzena finished paying and had put a dozen of the fruits into her bag and turned away from the stall when, suddenly, the boy dressed as a lion ran right into her arm hard enough to make her drop the bag. The cloudberries fell all over the ground, rolling away from her.

Alzena got to her knees and started trying to pick them up.

Over his shoulder, the boy shouted, "Sorry, lady!" and the boy dressed as a knight laughed and ran past as well.

Cato ran through the crowd as fast as he could. He got on his knees as well to help her find the cloudberries.

Cato was so busy looking at her fair skin, the few stray strands of her red hair, and her ice blue eyes that he didn't notice until he looked down that he was putting the cloudberries into his own pack.

Alzena and Cato both stopped what they were doing and looked at each other. Cato felt a thrill go over him as their eyes met. Alzena also felt something powerful, and for a moment, neither of them said anything. Then they both burst out laughing and Cato gave her the cloudberries back.

"That was…very kind of you," said Alzena. "Thank you so much for helping me."

"You're welcome. My name is Cato. It's a pleasure to meet you." He was surprised to find any words to say to her at all. They both stood up, not taking their eyes off each other, and smiling.

"I haven't seen you around the marketplace before," said Alzena. "Are you new here to Santara?" Looking at this man before her, she wondered how he got his confidence.

"Yes," said Cato. "I come from a land far away over the mountains named Farralina," Cato lied.

Alzena smiled at him anyway, and as she looked at him, she noticed over his shoulder a palace guard patrolling the marketplace. That could only mean one thing. Her father must be looking for her again, she realized. Alzena thought quickly.

"Since you've been so kind to me, I should show you the best spot in Santara to take in the view. Right now." She grabbed his hand and began leading him out of the marketplace, away from the guard.

"Right now?" asked Cato, following behind.

"Hey! You! Stop right there!"

Cato ran right alongside Alzena, not pausing for a second. Laughing, they took off through the marketplace, the knight banging his metal boots against the dirt as he ran behind them.

They bumped into some of the vendors, and even had to brush through crowds of customers. On their way to the gates, they ran so fast that the two kids that had been playing before had to dive out of the way to avoid being trampled.

The little kid with the wooden sword got right to his feet again and brandished the wooden sword, knocking it against the knight's armor and forcing him to stop.

"What do you think you're doing?" he asked as the boy started tugging on his leg. "Let go of me!"

"I'm going to feed you to the lion!" said the boy.

"Enough nonsense!" shouted the knight. "Stop that at once! Now see here! You've let them get away!"

Cato fled the marketplace, Alzena holding his hand. As they passed the gates and the flow of people began to dissipate, Alzena began to relax and walk slower. She led him up a long hill that reached a summit far above the marketplace. As they were walking, they continued to talk.

"Do you come to the marketplace very often?" asked Cato.

"Whenever I get the chance. It used to be my grandmother's favorite pastime to make cloudberry jam. Do you want a cloudberry? They are delicious."

Cato ate the cloudberry offered to him. A smile crossed his face. "I've never tasted anything like this before. The fruits in your land are juicy and delicious." Then he thought of something. "Where is your grandmother today? I didn't see her with you."

"That's because my grandmother died seven years ago," said Alzena.

Cato frowned. "I'm sorry to hear that."

As they reached the top of the hill, Cato could see for dozens of miles all around the great kingdom. Behind him in the distance was a great volcano, and below him, the deep green veil of the Forbidden Forest stretched out as far as he could see.

In the other direction, Cato could see the marketplace lights and the palace, looking small from so far away.

Beyond the palace and the marketplace lay the ocean and a harbor, which amazed Cato because he had never heard of the ocean before.

The boats in the harbor looked like little toy boats in the distance. But even at this distance, Cato could see the huge sails and the proud designs painted upon them in bright reds and blues and yellows. A proud yellow lion stood high above a great castle. His jaws were open in a tremendous roar, and a long white sword rose above his head, held high and strong to defend the castle below him, red bricks reaching down to the wide blue ocean below. The ocean represented the ocean around Santara, the castle represented the great castle of Santara, and the lion had always been the symbol defending Santara.

All those years in the Forbidden Forest, Cato had always been taught the legends of his ancestors. Eino's armor had been carefully preserved, and the image had been burned into his mind, every tiny detail matching the great sails he now watched billow in the coastal winds.

"That's the king's fleet out there in the harbor."

"Where I'm from, we have the same design, but on the armor it's faded. What were you saying?" Cato looked at Alzena, confused and distant, trying to pull himself back. "Did you say those were the queen's boats?"

"No," said Alzena, "the king controls this great fleet. The queen just takes care of the castle, and keeps all the servants cared for as well."

Cato realized how far up he was. He had to sit down just to take it all in.

Alzena sat down beside him. The sun was breaking through red clouds and shining over the entire land, pouring white and golden rays beneath the clouds and filling the air with light.

Alzena turned to him and said, "This is the view I was telling you about. Do you like it?"

Cato turned away from the view to look at her. "In all my life I have never seen such splendor. Way back in Farralina, there are so many trees you can't even see the sky sometimes. You don't know if it's day or night. But here the light shines brightly over everything."

Alzena smiled up at Cato, touching his hand. "I'm glad you like it."

"Like it?" said Cato. "It's the most amazing view I've ever seen. The whole world below us with not a tree anywhere to block our view, just these big rocks."

As Alzena smiled back at him, Cato turned to look at the view some more. He didn't notice the guard coming up the hill. Alzena did, though, and ran to hide behind a rock. Cato didn't notice her disappear because he was too busy looking at the view. Only a couple minutes later did he look away from the sun pouring over the land to see the guard approaching. He waited as the guard reached the top of the hill and finally got within speaking distance.

"Have you seen a woman with red hair up here?" asked the guard. He was stouter than the other guard, and not as assertive either. He was badly out of breath from the long climb up the hill.

"Nobody up here like that," answered Cato. "Just me." Cato gave the guard an imposing stare. The guard looked at Cato, saw a strong, well-dressed man that he didn't want to mess with, and said, "Well, then, good day." Then, after catching his breath, he continued. "Sorry to have bothered you."

The guard lifted his wide-brimmed hat politely, and Cato noticed the hair underneath was soaked in sweat. The guard turned back down the hill and retreated.

After the guard left, Cato looked around. He still couldn't see Alzena anywhere. He called her name a couple times, quietly, but when he looked around behind him, he noticed that the sun was getting very close to the horizon. It was almost time for him to change.

I need to get back to Kainuu, thought Cato. He headed off towards Kainuu's hut, which was a different way than the guard was going.

Chapter Eleven

Prince Yuli

Alzena continued to hide until she was sure the guard had left entirely. Once she came out from behind the rock, nobody else was up on the hill. She headed back towards the castle, coming in from the kitchen again.

The cook smiled and accepted her cloudberries.

Once she got into the hallway, though, she saw the same chubby prince, Prince Yuli, who was waiting for her before. She tried to move quickly past him, but Yuli grabbed the back of her hood and revealed her red hair.

Then he grabbed her arm. "Oh, that is you, Alzena! I finally caught you!"

Alzena jerked her arm away, trying to free herself. She looked at him, her face grimacing.

When he touched her, his skin was cold and clammy. His breath was very bad and his hair was scraggly and not well braided either.

In disgust she cried, "Get your filthy hands off of me!"

Prince Yuli did the opposite, reaching out fast and grabbing her hand hard and yanking her back towards him so close that his breath was overpowering. Alzena's knees bent, and she tried not to scream.

Prince Yuli leered with glee down at her and began twisting her wrist to make sure she was paying attention. Alzena continued to struggle and grunt. Prince Yuli hissed at her. He looked down his nose with contempt at her.

"Your father chose me to be your husband. You're going to belong to me pretty soon. You're going to do exactly as I say. Your father says I am to be the next king."

As Yuli continued to leer at her, she realized she had her other hand free. Without taking the time to give away her action, she slammed her other hand down on his wrist as hard as she could.

She felt something snap and felt a great rush of satisfaction, then even more relief as Yuli let go of her arm and retreated a step backwards, massaging his wrist.

He glared at Alzena. She glared right back.

Since he didn't look like he was about to hurt her, Alzena took a moment to speak.

"I'm not going to marry anybody out of duty! I want to marry out of love. And I'll never belong to anybody! And if you ever touch me like that again, ever, you're going back home with one hand!"

Alzena stormed off down the hallway back towards her room. Prince Yuli watched her leave, and then stormed off in the other direction, towards the king's chambers.

Yuli found the king's chambers unguarded, because all the guards were out looking for Princess Alzena. He threw open the door with a bang, and entered boldly.

"Your Highness, the Princess Alzena has been avoiding me for days. Now I find her, and she rejects me. And she tried to break my wrist. I can't abide for a woman like that! I'm leaving right now!"

Yuli turned to leave. King Pajari raised both of his arms above his head and slammed his foot down on the floor with a crash.

"Wait!"

Yuli froze in his tracks and whirled around to face the angry king.

"Wait, wait, wait! You can't just come in here without knocking and tell me you're going! My guards have been looking for Alzena all day and I'll make her answer for what she's done. Come back, we can work something out!"

Yuli scoffed at the king. "You need to work something out with your daughter! There's something wrong with her! She doesn't act like a woman! Women need to know their place!"

As he left, he slammed the door.

Yuli returned to his room and commanded the servants to begin packing.

King Pajari stood inside his chambers, breathing heavily. Part of him was angry with Alzena, but part of him was scared of what the other nobles would say about her behavior.

As King Pajari continued to stare at the door, the black shadow of mist formed behind him again.

The evil voice stirred inside his mind again, and, this time, he listened even more carefully. He knew the voice had been right to choose Prince Yuli. Sunray Island was a powerful land, quite a large island, in fact, that had amassed many riches for having the best blankets in the entire realm.

Also, thanks to Yuli, the king realized, the truth about Alzena had come to the surface. The voice was giving him useful advice.

"Are you going to let your daughter get away with that?" whispered the voice. "Who wants a king that can't even control his own daughter? They will say you are a coward. She disobeyed you. You've got to put her in her place."

The king nodded. Underneath his breath, he muttered, "I will put her in her place."

"You don't understand. You don't see the whole picture." The whispering in his mind grew more insistent. "She wants to take the throne from you. Soon she will take away everything you hold dear. She's probably been planning for months."

The king looked out the window. As he watched, he saw Prince Yuli and his servants leaving on horseback. He could see the common people talking to each other in whispers.

"They're talking about you," said the whisper. "They're saying you're getting weak, you're all washed up. Don't lose control of your kingdom."

"Shut up!" screamed King Pajari.

"My king?" asked Lydia. "What's going on?"

"Alzena came back, just like you said she would. But she broke Prince Yuli's wrist and she's hiding in the castle. Look, there he goes now!"

King Pajari pointed out the window. Lydia hesitated, but the shaking arm pointing out the window told her that the king was running out of patience.

She walked over to the window and looked outside. As Prince Yuli rode away, he turned back to the castle and threw some malevolent punches into the air their way as he left. Then he turned around and rode proudly away from the castle.

King Pajari boiled with rage.

"Alzena is going to bring shame to the entire Kingdom of Santara! Tell the servants to bring her here at once."

Queen Lydia turned around. "I'll tell her myself. She's embarrassed us once too often."

"No!" said King Pajari. "I don't trust you! You always take her side. In fact," he said, "I don't trust you at all." Turning to the door, he cried "Servants!" Once the servants had entered, he told them, "Bring Princess Alzena to my chambers at once!"

"Not the Throne Room?" asked the servant.

"Where everyone can see me? Not on your life! Have her brought to my chamber immediately. Now get out of here!"

The servants left, closing the door behind them. Lydia walked to the other side of the room, toward the door.

"You're staying right here," said King Pajari. "You seem to have a problem remembering your place too."

Lydia stiffened, but remained where she was. "You've changed, Pajari. You're not the same anymore."

King Pajari scoffed. "What do you care?"

Chapter Twelve

The Tower

Alzena was still getting out of her yellow dress when there was a knock at the door from a servant. "My lady?" asked the servant.

Alzena finished removing her clothing and began putting on her royal garments.

"Not right now," she said. "Can it wait?"

"My lady, no, my lady. The king is furious. He wants to speak with you right away."

As Alzena got dressed, she called back, "Just let me get my hair done. I'm almost ready." Done changing, she opened the door, letting the servant in.

The servant waited at the doorway, beckoning to the princess.

"Oh, I know what he wants," said Alzena. "It's probably because I chased off another suitor he handpicked for me. He is so predictable!"

"But, my lady, you must come at once. I've never seen the king so angry before."

"Well, I suppose I'd better go see him." She walked with the servant over to the king's chambers.

King Pajari stood in his chambers, next to Queen Lydia and the servants. Alzena stood before them, and she noticed two guards come in and stand on each side of her.

She could tell right away that her father was beside himself with anger. King Pajari's hands were clenching into fists so tightly that the knuckles were turning white from the loss of blood.

"You have disobeyed me for the last time!" he shouted. "I have no choice—I have to send you to the Tower Cell until you learn your lesson!"

Queen Lydia had not realized the king was going to do that. She cried out, "King Pajari, no! That's our daughter!"

The king was so mad that he turned on his own wife. "Quiet, woman!" he ordered. The king hit Queen Lydia with a powerful backhand across the face. The queen fell to the floor, with her hand covering her face. She began to sob. As her hand fell away, Alzena could see that her nose was bleeding from the force of the king's blow.

Alzena began crying herself and found the strength to escape the guards, who were holding her with less force because they were shocked at what had happened too. Alzena ran over to the queen.

"It will be all right, Mother," she said, crying. "Father, I won't fight them."

The palace nanny ran over to help Queen Lydia get to her feet. As Alzena watched her mother get up slowly, the guards came to each side of her and began lifting her up to be taken away. Alzena hung her head with sorrow, and then suddenly snapped out of it, realizing the king would come to his senses and free her soon. She stood straight and proud, and Alzena allowed herself to be marched out by the guards with her head held high.

Behind her, in the chamber, King Pajari waited until the guards had left, looked at the servants and the queen all quietly staring at him, and stormed out of the room, slamming the door behind him.

As Alzena and the guard walked up the long spiral stone staircase that led to the top of the highest tower, she struggled and groaned in pain. It was very hard work climbing so many steep stairs, and her knees felt swollen and burning from exertion. The guard looked at her with sympathy. The other guard had felt too guilty about imprisoning Princess Alzena, and had left the younger guard to do the hard work all by himself.

The guard confirmed her suspicions. "I don't want to do this. Everyone loves you here at the castle. I've never seen his Majesty act that way before."

Alzena looked back at him with sympathy, and the guard was surprised to see no anger revealed in her face.

"It's all right," said Alzena. "I know you're just doing your duty."

They reached the top of the staircase. At the top was an old rusty wooden door. Inside was the most forbidding dungeon cell of all—the Tower Cell, where no one could survive the fall, even if there was any way to escape. The guard escorted her inside.

He treated her with care and placed his hand on her back to guide her.

Alzena shrank from his touch and entered the cell. The guard closed the door, and then paused outside to draw a long, slow breath. Then he composed himself and locked the door with a clang. He began walking down the stairs, sniffling.

The cell was dark and cold and covered in drops of moisture. One narrow crack in the wall served as a window. This small and misshapen crack only allowed a small view of outside, but not even enough room to put her hand through to feel the fresh air. Through the window she could see the gloom after sunset. In the darkness outside, Alzena saw two dark shadows running in the direction of the Forbidden Forest.

"It must have been my imagination," said Alzena.

Then she lay down on the cold stone floor in the corner, confused and upset. As she drifted off to sleep, she quietly wept.

Cato got back to Kainuu's hut dangerously near sunset. "I found a beautiful woman at the marketplace and we had a great time together. This world is amazing and beautiful."

"Don't get too close to them," he whispered. "That will only lead to heartbreak. They don't understand us when we change. Let's get inside quickly. There's only fifteen minutes before we change. We can't be seen."

When they got inside, and were eating fish soup for extra nutrition before the change, Cato spoke to Kainuu again. "You know, I really think you'd be happy if you came to see your family again. They really miss you. Your mother thinks you're gone forever. We should show them that it is possible to leave the Forbidden Forest without being killed. Besides, you said you don't really like it here."

Kainuu was happy. He seemed to have changed his mind. "After all this time," he said, "it would be a joyous reunion. I shall return with you for now. But I cannot abandon my lures and my lines for too long."

As they went to an open area in the hut to transform, they left their clothing behind on the chairs so it wouldn't be torn. As their muscles began to stretch and expand, they both fell to their hands and knees as their joints popped and their bones stretched. They roared in agony.

Completely transformed, they went running across the fields in sheer joy, the same two shadows that Alzena saw from her tower window.

By the time they entered the Forbidden Forest, it was completely dark out and all the lion-people were already in lion-form. One silvery old female, Kainuu's mother, came out of the pack first and spoke with her mind. *"My son, my son, I'm so glad to see you again."* As lions do, they rubbed their faces together in greeting.

Lena, Cato's mother, was much slower in greeting Cato, but grudgingly she came over and finally nuzzled his face. *"You came back to me."*

Lena and Kainuu's mother both yawned with happiness, releasing deep growls of pleasure, and Cato and Kainuu began to smile.

"We made the right choice," said Kainuu.

"It's a beautiful world out there, but there's no place like this forest," answered Cato.

Chapter Thirteen

The Escape

Queen Lydia snuck out of bed and listened carefully for the sound of foot-steps passing her door, but heard nothing but her own hushed breathing. The king's study was just down the hall and down towards the alcove.

The king slept in an entirely different chamber, far distant from his study or the queen. Lydia had long since given up hope that the king would ever sleep near her again.

As she left, she saw the palace nanny roaming the halls.

Queen Lydia motioned for her to come over, and Margaret silently approached.

When Margaret was nearby, the queen whispered to her, "I'm going to help Alzena escape. Pajari has gone too far this time. Go get some food and some clothing for Alzena, but hurry."

"I have an idea where she can go where she'll be safe," said Margaret. "She can go to Masala's village."

"That's a great idea," whispered the queen. "Bring a map so she can find her way."

Then she went to the king's study, which was locked. She brought out her collection of keys and opened the door. She had made a wax copy of the key years ago, but the king had never found out about it.

Inside the study were many books, but the entire place was dark. She knew exactly where the desk was and about the secret drawer on the side; she felt for the trick handle, hidden because it was flat and looked like the rest of the desk. One area of the wood, however, was much smoother, and she soon discovered that spot. She pressed there, and the drawer opened. She grabbed the keys to the tower and left.

Outside, Queen Lydia looked around for anybody spying on her, and quickly went down the hallway towards the linens. She met Margaret, already returning.

"I've got the key, let's go," she whispered, but it was hard to keep the excitement out of her voice.

"Not yet!" said Margaret. "Let me finish packing this first!" She continued to stuff clothing into the bundle while Queen Lydia looked from side to side.

"Hurry, would you? There, now put the map in there and let's get moving."

They went up the stairs, the queen moving swiftly, Margaret struggling up the steep stairs that went seven stories into the air.

At the top, the queen waited for Margaret in the stillness, and put her ear to the door. She could hear Alzena breathing, and exhaled a slow sigh of relief.

Once Margaret got there, breathing heavier, the queen opened the door to Alzena's cell and entered. One look at her daughter trapped in that cold, damp cell made her feel sick in her stomach. She shook her daughter awake.

Alzena was overjoyed to see her mother and her nanny, having felt so miserable before.

"What are you doing here?" she asked.

"We're getting you out of here!" said the queen.

"There's a village far away where you can be safe," said Margaret. "It's deep inside the Forbidden Forest. Your father will never think of looking for you there."

"Why would you do this for me? What if Father hurts you, Mother? I don't want anything to happen to you because of me." She began to cry.

The queen answered, "Child, I wouldn't know what I would do if anything happened to you. Go, be safe, I'll be fine. I can take care of myself and most of these guards are still on my side, except for Dax and Bruno. But please, just go. Here's a cloak so no one will see you go, and some food and clothing for your journey."

Margaret also sat down next to Alzena. "In your things, I put a map of how to get to Masala's village. Don't lose it. I've been there before, and there's nowhere else as safe in all of Santara."

Alzena said, "I don't know how I can ever repay you. Is there anything I can do?"

The queen said, "Just take care of yourself, child, and when you get there, tell them that the king is out of his mind and you need their protection. Masala and his people will take care of you."

After walking down the steps and outside of the palace, Alzena hugged her mother and her nanny goodbye, and wrapped in the cloak, quietly escaped into the gloom, moving from tree to tree to stay completely hidden.

As she got further from the palace, she had only the light of the stars to guide her. Even in the meadows and farmland, it was hard to see, and Alzena was almost invisible in the darkness.

She trembled from the cold and the wind pulled at her cloak and chilled her arms until the muscles felt like rocks. Every sound made her flinch and back away.

Sometime deep in the night the meadows gave way to a black wall of trees. The edge of the Forbidden Forest loomed before her.

Before she entered the forest, she flashed back on all the stories she heard as a child about the monsters that lived in the Forbidden Forest, black, sooty, dangerous things with many claws.

But then she looked back at the castle far away, with its lights shining even to the edge of the Forbidden Forest, and she remembered that her nanny and her mother were looking out for her, and would never send her into danger. "Besides," she whispered, her teeth chattering, "those are just folktales anyway." Then she disappeared into the forest.

Alzena walked through the dark, feeling with her hands for somewhere safe and hidden to lie down for the night. She heard a low growling.

Already half-frozen, she could see red beady eyes in the dark and froze with fear. Snapping sounds and flashes of static electricity revealed razor sharp fangs far below. The monster had to be gigantic to possess such a large head.

"Oh no, the stories are true!"

She flailed around in a panic, turned to run away, and made exactly two steps away from the pursuing monster before she hit her head on a branch in the darkness, hard. She saw nothing but stars, and she knew they weren't the ones in the sky. She turned around unsteadily.

With her vision fading, Alzena saw a huge shadow leap up and attack the creature as she fell to the ground. She could still hear faintly, and her mouth felt cold and metallic. What she heard through the ringing in her head was a whimpering, and then a chewing, and then she remembered nothing.

Chapter Fourteen

The Lions' Choice

Cato pulled away from the bear he had killed in the forest, seeing clearly even in the pitch black with his enhanced vision as a lion. Cato paused, put his head to the beast's chest, and listened carefully. There was no more blood pumping through its heart anymore. It lay cold and still in the forest.

Cato let out a long roar of victory, and as it trailed off, he looked to the side of him and saw Alzena, unconscious, in the bushes. He ran over to her and put his head to her chest as well.

Alzena's heart still pumped, but the pulse was very slow and he could barely hear the thumping ventricles. He kept listening, and despite its weakness, the heartbeat somehow persisted, stubbornly beating, not giving up yet.

Cato let out another long, high-pitched, painful roar, and before long, all the other lions were running to him, strong legs padding in the moonlight, males and females.

Some of the males were more curious, leaning forward and sniffing Alzena's new scent, the females finding offense and backing away.

The oldest lion in the village spoke up. *"I have never heard of a human entering the Forbidden Forest."*

"A human?" said Lena. *"What do we do now?"*

"This woman needs our help!" said Cato.

"She's an outsider," another lion hissed. All the other lions growled in agreement.

"We are exiles too," said Kainuu, and the lone lion remained silent after that. He flicked his tail in frustration a few times, and so did some of the others, but all the lions respected Kainuu, for he had ventured beyond the Forbidden Forest

and survived, and the flicking slowly subsided.

"We need to get the medicine man," said Cato. *"I'll remain here and protect her. Go to Masala's village and tell them to get here as quickly as possible. She's badly injured."*

"I'm the fastest," said Kainuu.

"Yes, you are, Kainuu. I ran beside you on the way back here. You are even faster than me. I trust you. Now hurry!"

Kainuu ran swiftly through the forest, his keen sense of smell guiding him through the forest even better than his piercing eyes. As he ran, his lungs began to ache and torture him, but he never paused once.

As he got to Masala's village, he saw the little huts ringed in a circle around the campfire in the center of the village.

The people of Masala's village were lions all the time, day and night, for their humanity was lost entirely. Every villager had thick fur and long whiskers, and stared with pride at Kainuu.

The chief had the largest mane of all, and a wide nose that spoke of experience and wisdom.

The lions separated as Kainuu approached the fire, and the chief approached him from the other side. "You approach us with respect, but it is late at night. Why do you come here now?" asked the chief.

"I need to speak with your medicine man. Someone's hurt," said Kainuu.

"Come into the hut with me," said the chief, and Kainuu went into where an ancient shriveled medicine man waited in the shadows. Kainuu knew their medicine man was very powerful, and bent his head down to the floor in reverence.

"A human woman has entered the Forbidden Forest. These are strange times. The tides are turning, and now a woman needs your aid. She needs your help, or she may die."

"I will come right away," answered the medicine man, raising his bony, ancient frame to its full height. "A human entering the Forbidden Forest—this is unheard of. Take me to her immediately!" They left the hut and hurried through the forest.

They arrived where Alzena had fallen. The medicine man looked at her carefully, and said, "She is freezing and she has some bad cuts on her head, and some swelling. If she's not brought into a cabin by a fire soon she will die. Do any of you have a cabin nearby that will work?"

"Mine is the closest," said Lena. "I'll take you there now."

The medicine man carefully picked up Alzena after wrapping her in a woven blanket and walked through the forest. He carried Alzena into Lena's hut carefully, and laid her on the bed. Then he stoked the fire until it was very warm in the cabin. Several of the other lions followed inside, talking amongst each other.

"Why is he taking care of the outsider?" said one.

"I hope she didn't see you change," said another.

"What if she did?" worried another one.

"What if she tells the other humans about us?" asked another.

"What if they come and hunt us down?" cried Lena.

"Calm down, don't do anything rash," said Cato. "Let's make sure she's okay first, and then once she wakes up, you will get all the answers you're looking for. I'll make sure that all your questions are answered. Leave now, let her rest, and when she is awake and feeling better, I'll talk to her and find out exactly what's going on. Then we will have a civilized discussion about what to do. But now is not the time. Go home. Now."

Cato made sure everyone but the medicine man had left, who was still applying compresses to her bruised head and cleaning her cuts.

Eventually, the medicine man had done all he could and left her alone to rest with Cato still standing guard. Once the medicine man had left, Cato lay down next to the bed to watch over Alzena as she slept peacefully.

Chapter Fifteen

Masala's Village

In the morning, Cato changed back into a human. It was not as painful as turning into a lion, but painful nonetheless as bones shortened, muscles shriveled, and fur pulled back under the skin, making him itch all over. He looked over at Alzena and saw she was still asleep but recovering. As she rested, Cato whittled a small piece of wood into the likeness of a fox. He burrowed a secret compartment inside the sculpture so it would be practical.

The pink flush of blood had returned to her pale skin. He got dressed and stepped outside the hut, where he saw right away several of the Lion-People standing nearby trying to look like they were doing something else. Lena came over to him, not hiding her concern or disdain, and started asking him questions.

"So who is this woman anyway, and would you like to tell me how she ended up in the forest?"

Cato looked back at his mother. "She's still asleep, for one thing. But I can tell you who she is. She's a woman I met in the marketplace in this land beyond the forest, the land they call Santara."

"But don't they do something when people disappear? What if someone comes looking for her?"

"Relax, Mother. I'm sure everything will be fine. Once we get her back to health, I'm sure she will want to get back to Santara. But first she needs to heal. She still hasn't woken up yet."

Alzena wasn't actually asleep. She listened as Cato and Lena argued outside the window, so when he came back inside, she quickly shut her eyes and pretended to still be asleep. She tried very hard not to move her face at all, even though the presence of Cato in the room woke up all of her senses at once.

Cato could see her lip trembling, however, so he was pretty sure she was awake. He slowly washed her forehead, where the bleeding had finally stopped. Very, very slowly, she opened one of her eyes.

Cato stopped touching her forehead and moved back a little.

Alzena looked directly at him with both eyes open and said, "Cato, is that you?"

Cato answered her softly. "Yes. My people were wandering the forest when I heard your cries. I came to your rescue. That was very dangerous what you did. We have bears here in the forest. You could have been killed."

Alzena looked around and tried to sit up. When she got her head off the pillow, a strong wave of dizziness and nausea came over her and she put her head back down.

"Where are we?"

"In my village, deep in the Forbidden Forest. You're bruised up, and there's a bad cut on your head. You need at least a couple days to recover."

Alzena felt her forehead and groaned with pain as soon as she touched the cut on her head. "No wonder I've been so dizzy. Thank you so much for your kindness. At the very least I guess I owe you an explanation of why I left in such a hurry the other day and how I came to be in the forest."

Cato answered, "Never mind that now. First you need rest and food. This soup is what my mother always made for me when I wasn't feeling well." He went over to the fire and poured a big mug of peppermint tea from the kettle. "Here, have some. You need your strength."

Alzena smelled the tea from across the room, and as he brought it to her lips, she drank. "This tea tastes even better than it smells."

Cato looked at her, surprised. "I'm glad you like it. This was a recipe handed down for hundreds of years."

Alzena looked around the cabin, stopping when she saw the window. "I love the flowers on your curtains!"

Cato was aware she'd changed the subject, but he was too proud of his work to avoid answering her. "Here, the hot tea is easier to digest. You need all the warmth you can get. You were so cold last night we thought we were going to lose you. Now have some more tea."

"Oh, how did that table get carved with those animals?" asked Alzena. "Did you do that, Cato? That's magnificent!"

"Yes, that's what I do. I've been a woodcarver all my life. I have to do something out here in the forest." Cato asked, "Have you still got a headache?"

"No, that tea is making me feel so much better," said Alzena. "What I really need is some fresh air."

As Cato and Alzena emerged, she noticed out of the corner of her eye several of Cato's friends disappear into the forest. Alzena tried to pretend she hadn't seen it.

Cato had seen them, however, and was tired of being stared at. "I know a place we can go with a waterfall," he said under his breath. "Let's go there."

She smiled and said, "Yes, I'd love to." As they walked into the forest, she occasionally heard branches breaking in the brush, but those sounds got more and more distant as time went by. Wildflowers and butterflies were all around, and down by the water's edge, as the footpath followed a stream, the flowers grew more vividly than she'd ever seen in the meadows. By that point, she heard no one following them anymore.

Eventually, the trail led away from the water down around some steeper slopes, but when they reached the bottom, she heard a steady whooshing sound like air being let out of a bellows. As she got past the trees into the clearing, she could see a gigantic waterfall pouring down the sides of the rock in every crevice and splitting into sprays of rainbows in clouds of mist against the rocks that still jutted out. A bubbling pool spread out below.

"These are healing waters!" Cato said over the roar of the waterfall. "Come with me!"

He went into the water and Alzena followed him. It was extremely warm, which she didn't expect. Millions of bubbles rose from the water, kissing her skin in thousands of tickles. It was truly healing, and all of her fatigue and pain melted away. Cato came up close to her and gently pulled her hair back to keep it out of the water. The birthmark of a swan on the back of her neck was exposed.

"The royal birthmark!" he said. "Just like me!" He turned around and pulled back his hair to show Alzena his own proof of royalty. "This mark was handed down to me from my ancestors, the royal men who entered this forest so long ago. No doubt your histories still tell of them."

Alzena did remember the stories her grandmother had told her. "Our history does tell of three people that were exiled for betraying the kingdom, but the details have been lost to history."

Cato sighed, but thought twice about arguing. "That's not exactly what happened. We have a lot to talk about. But first I want to know why you left. You still haven't told me. If you're ready, I'm listening."

Alzena suddenly felt very flushed and climbed out of the pool. She sat down on a rock and Cato sat next to her. "It's a long story, but I suppose you have to know. I ran away last night because I was hiding from my father. My father happens to be King Pajari. My favorite person had always been my grandmother. I loved her more than anything. After she passed away, my father became bitter, and all he ever talked to me about was getting married and being responsible. He tried to take all the happiness out of my life. And now he's losing his mind."

"What did he do?"

"He ordered me locked up in the high tower until I obeyed him. He wants me to marry one of these suitors, but none of them treat me with any kindness or respect. Thankfully my mother and a friend helped me escape." Alzena began to softly cry.

Cato leaned closer and wiped the tears away from her face with gentleness. "As long as you're under my protection, no harm will come to you," he said. "But you know it will take some time for my people to trust you."

"There is something else, now that you mention that." She pulled out a map where the village was marked with an X in the forest. "Can you get me to this village?" she asked. "I heard it was safe for me there."

Cato studied it, and suddenly was extremely curious. "That village," he said. "For anyone to know of it, they must have come from there themselves. That village is completely hidden and veiled. Nobody knows about it. How did you come to find out about it?"

"Take me there and I'll tell you the whole story," she said. "That way we both get something, all right?"

"Agreed," said Cato. "But before we go, I have to warn you. They look different than you and me, so don't be scared. They don't mean any harm."

Alzena said, "As long as you're next to me, Cato, I trust you."

"Let's go then. We have to go through the waterfall to get to the cave." Alzena walked back into the warm bubbling water, following Cato. As they got closer to the waterfall, the sound got louder and louder until it was deafening. As they went under the waterfall, Cato put his arm over her head to shield her, but she was still blasted by huge gushes of water as she went through. Alzena felt baptized by the strength of the water.

Then they were on the other side and the rumbling of the waterfall was echoing through the cave. Many years ago, the villagers had put a few lanterns in to light the way. Only after traveling away from the waterfall into the darkness did she see any light at all as her eyes tried to adjust. As they ventured through, the rumbling grew quieter and quieter until all she could hear was their footfalls on the rocky floor. As daylight appeared at the other end of the cave, they walked quicker until they emerged in Masala's village.

Alzena was in shock, even though she was trying to prepare for anything. People with faces like lions peered back at her. Even the women's were furry. Long whiskers stuck out and tiny noses were flattened against jaws filled with razor-sharp teeth. Their eyes were all green. Alzena was terrified, for she had been taught to fear lions all her life.

But as she looked closer, she noticed they were all standing upright.

"What happened to all of you?" she asked.

They bowed, and she looked around and noticed the chief approaching. He was dressed head to toe in beaded work. The people began chanting, "Masala! Masala! Masala!" and Princess Alzena bowed with Cato and the rest of them as he approached.

"Please, come to my hut where we can sit in privacy and talk," said Masala. As they walked over to the chief's hut, Alzena noticed that the round structures were intricately detailed with designs she'd never seen before. Fresh flowers and plants bloomed in every direction, and she was amazed by how beautiful the village was.

The hut of the chief was larger than the others and ornately decorated in many colors.

The chief said, "Please, come inside, and all your questions will be answered. I have a few of my own as well."

Alzena went inside behind Cato, and found herself urged to sit by the round table in the center of the room while the chief sat on the other side and stared at Alzena very carefully for a few minutes.

"How did you know about this village? Now, before you answer, you must know that our existence is a dark secret."

"My nanny, Margaret, at the palace."

"Margaret! I knew it. When she was very young, we found a child wandering in the woods. That was dozens of years ago. We named her Margaret because she was too young to remember her name."

"So how did she end up at the palace as my nanny?"

"That I cannot tell. You would have to ask the people of the royal palace to learn that. But we took care of her, and I am glad she rewarded our care by trusting you with the knowledge of us. But ever since this curse has fallen on us, we have been exiles. Although Cato and his people become human during the day, we are like this all the time. We never get to change back." The chief fell silent, thoughtful.

"All this time," said Alzena, "I thought it was just a fairytale told to children to keep them good. I never imagined it would all be true. To be turned into lions, exiled to the forest."

"So, Princess, how shall I address you?" He bowed before her.

"How did you know I'm a princess?"

"You mentioned the palace, and the whole kingdom is talking about Princess Alzena's escape."

"Oh, please, no," she said. "It is just Alzena now. King Pajari has lost his mind. He had me locked up in the tower. My mother and Margaret, they helped me escape, said I'd be safe here. It's not safe for me there anymore."

"I wonder what happened to Pajari," said the chief. "His mind was said to be very strong." He turned to Cato. "It sounds like she's back again."

"What do you mean she? What are you talking about?" asked Alzena.

"The Evil Sorceress," said the chief. "She revels in making good people do horrible things. I'm afraid the only thing that can stop her is the Goddess of Light. There were once two sacred books, one for light magic and one for dark magic, but they've been lost to us for hundreds of years."

"I do know that part. They always told me in the palace how the library was locked up and forbidden to enter, but I found a way to get a copy of the key, so I can get in. I know from the old stories where they are. Just think, Cato, this could help my father, and it might even help you."

"I don't believe anything will ever lift this curse, but if it can save your father and restore order to the kingdom, then it's worth trying," said Cato. "Just don't let anything happen to you."

It was starting to get dark by the time they emerged from the chief's hut. Cato began to get nervous. He hadn't realized how late it had become.

"I wish so bad I could be there with you, but these are my people. You're the princess. You need to be out in that world."

"Look, the sun is barely setting, let's talk some more."

"But, Alzena, I have to go. I'm about to change. I don't want to accidentally hurt you."

Alzena came over and hugged him. "I know in my heart you won't. You're a good man, Cato—human or beast." She lifted his downturned head with her gentle hand. "Your heart is so pure, no evil could ever penetrate it. Please trust me. Let me see the other side of you. Let's sit over by the lake."

They did so. "It's not going to be pretty. It causes me intense pain. But don't be scared. I'll be fine." As the sun sank below the horizon, Cato became more worried as the time of transformation drew closer. He walked away from Alzena a good distance and waited for a few moments. Within seconds, his body began to change, and as the curse took hold, he felt energy tugging through his body, as it did every night. But he had never changed in front of a human, and his instincts to fear them kicked in. He began to shake, feeling exposed.

By the lakeshore, Alzena saw him transforming in the twilight He roared in agony as his clothing tore, and Alzena watched helplessly as he was wracked with pain. She couldn't stand the helpless feeling anymore, and she began moving closer to him in sympathy.

Cato raised his arms over his head and roared. He saw Alzena and turned away to run.

Alzena cried out, "No, Cato, please, I'm not afraid."

Cato felt relief and stopped roaring. He eventually breathed deeply, completely transformed, and looked at her again. For a moment, he panicked again and panted, but his eyes began to narrow in relaxation as he recognized her. He nuzzled her face with his head. She ran her fingers down his mane and the fur on his back as gently as touching a baby.

"Cato, you're the most beautiful lion I've ever seen, and I love you as a lion or a man." They walked off together into a quiet spot by the trees and he nestled his body into the grass. She snuggled in next to him. Silently, they fell asleep together, his body heat keeping her warm all night long.

The next morning, she put her cloak around Cato because, as a human already, he was naked and shivering. He woke up feeling warmer, but said nothing for a while, just looked at her.

They went down to the hut and got dressed. Afterwards, Lena came in and said, "My, good morning, princess! You must be starving." Soon the smell of roasting flatbread, savory meats, and fresh cheese filled the kitchen. Cato went into the back while breakfast was being made up and brought out a beautiful wooden fox he'd carved for her with a secret compartment that he showed her how to open to hide the key. "Just in case you get caught," he said.

"I know my way around my castle. I'll be safe, my love."

Cato grabbed the back of her neck and drew her into a kiss. She felt tingling all along her spine, and she thought she would faint right into his strong arms. "Be careful, my love," he whispered, and her trembling stopped as a rush of confidence came over her.

After breakfast, she left the forest but took her time so she would return to the castle when it was already dark so no one would see her.

Chapter Sixteen

The Library

Alzena, safely inside the walls of the palace without being spotted, tiptoed to the closet where a staircase spiraled down. The closet was never talked about anymore, but her grandmother had told her many old stories about it and she had already opened that door a couple of times just to make sure the stairs were actually there. The second time, she had dared to go down before she heard someone and decided against exploring further. Then she had made the copy of the key.

She took the key out of the compartment in the fox and continued silently down the stone stairs. As she heard footsteps echoing down below her, she stopped and ducked behind a post, then realized the echoes were playing tricks on her and it was just a skittering mouse running past. Shivering only partly from cold, she finished descending and stood in front of the two imposing wooden doors. Nothing marked them out of the ordinary except how massive they were. They had been down here under the castle for more than 400 years, and all kinds of knowledge lay hidden behind them.

She inserted the key in the lock and turned it. With a massive groan, the doors opened wide, the candlelight she carried revealing row upon row of scrolls and bookshelves as far as she could see.

The great library was once again illuminated. She heard screeches and clicking as bats and mice scurried for shelter, disturbed as their 200-year long seclusion was broken. She noticed the ones that ran past her were albino, sucked clean of all color from the pitch-blackness of their isolation.

Alzena began exploring the shelves. The candlelight illuminated the tapestries on the bookcases, and she cleaned the centuries of dust off them with the sleeve of her dress. One by one, she read the tapestries as she passed the bookshelves, her voice the only thing that broke the silence in hushed whispers.

"History, art, plants." She kept moving. "This is not the right area," she said to herself. She went deeper into the bowels of the library.

The candlelight shone on an ornate pair of double doors covered in gold in the back, and she increased her pace, knowing what she was heading for now.

With all her weight on the latch, it released slowly, stiff from years of rustiness. When it finally broke free, a cloud of dust escaped. She covered her mouth, but still coughed quietly in the gloom.

Recovering, she moved inside, where several sacred texts had been stored before the vault had been closed forever. "The Secret of Alchemy," read one, and she noticed a white book, then a black book with claws on it.

She approached the black book, but something inside her pulled her back, some instinct that smelled danger. She moved down the table and touched another book, the one she was looking for. She could tell just by the way the magic shivered under her hand when she touched the surface. She carefully brushed away the dust to reveal *The Art of Magic and Curses Used During the Reign of King Aro—A Complete Collection.*

Touching the book carefully so it wouldn't break, Alzena lifted it and opened it up to find the spells and knowledge she was looking for. Dust flew everywhere and she coughed violently, extinguishing the candle. Alzena had never experienced darkness this complete, and she was petrified for a few seconds entombed in the depths of this ancient library of knowledge.

Then she found her tinder and struck it a few times until she had managed to light the candle again. Able to see again, she placed the book in her bag and walked out of the library, eager to be gone from that forsaken place with everything she needed to make her father sane and break the curse,

After making it safely up the stairs, Alzena was horrified to hear metal boot steps marching down the hallway and knew for sure it was a guard. She blew out the candle, then held her breath. Noticing the nearest column, she slid behind it before the guard noticed anything amiss.

She continued the rest of her departure by moonlight, and from the few candles in the palace, followed the corridors to her exit. She made it out across the fields to where her new friends awaited her return in the Forbidden Forest.

By the time she had made the long journey back to the forest, it was still night. Alzena called for Cato and they went inside.

Once they were settled, Alzena began reading the book to him. "This ancient knowledge says that the Curse of the Lions is an extremely powerful spell. It's incredibly strong. It says that only death itself can break the spell and release the lions from the humans. But there is hope still, because there's more."

"There is another way?"

"It says here that there is another way. The Goddess of Fire, who dwells on a mountain called Ravensblood, is named Uta, according to these wizards. Only she can break the curse that binds you together without anyone having to die."

Cato looked at her hopefully.

Alzena continued. "Three flowers are sacred to Uta. They are the Chrysanthemum for its great bloom, the Forsythia for its steadfastness, and Ravensblood flowers for the mountain that is her home. The Ravensblood will show the seeker the way. The Goddess of Fire even has the power to destroy the Evil Sorceress and can even heal those who have lost their minds! We've got to find her!"

Cato thought for a second, tapping his paw and taking a moment to take in the phase of the moons. "That Ravensblood will be blooming tomorrow!" he spoke. "I have to hurry."

Alzena said, "But can't I come with you?"

Cato answered, "No, this is my journey. I understand the meaning behind these words you tell me. If there is a death to occur, it will be the death of the beast inside of me. This is my journey, and mine alone to make. I can't risk your life as well. I don't want to see you get hurt."

"I can take care of myself. Cato, I'm the only one who knows where it's at," argued Alzena.

Cato answered, "Then draw for me a map so I can travel there safely and tell me everything else I need to know."

Deep into the night, straight into the golden light of dawn when the clouds were flaming red and the sky was an orchestra of color, Alzena continued reading to Cato. When Cato had everything he needed to know, he went outside and saddled the brown and white horse Kainuu let him borrow.

Before he left, Cato turned around to hug and kiss Alzena goodbye. He put his hands on her shoulders and said, "I've got to hurry now. My thoughts of you will see me through the journey. I'll win the Goddess's favor and return to you to set all this right again. Until we meet again, my love."

Alzena stood there watching him ride off into the distance. She went after him for a step or two, and then caught herself with a grunt. Massaging her shoulders and retreating to the hut, she collapsed at the table, crying with her head in her hands. Kainuu brought some tea over and tried to comfort her, but she spit it out at once. "I know he is very strong and brave. He will make it through these trials, princess."

Alzena smelled a pungent odor and knew it was a foul omen. She looked around for the smell, even sniffing the tea, but finding no source made her panic more.

"No!" she sobbed. "He's going to die out there and I'll never see him again. I've got a bad feeling about this. I've got to stop him." She fought Kainuu off, even though he tried to keep her there, and ran out the front door. Kainuu stood there, watching her, helpless.

Alzena's legs burned as she ran, but she didn't pay them any heed. She kept wiping the tears out of her eyes to see clearly.

Chapter Seventeen

The Death of the King

Alzena was walking along the fields, looking for Cato. She heard horse hoofs come up behind her, but didn't stop until she heard a voice cry, "Princess Alzena!"

She turned around, too surprised to deny it. "Yes?" She realized it was a palace guard, but he was crying, which surprised Alzena even more. Guards were trained not to cry by her unforgiving father.

"What's going on?" said Alzena. "The guards are never supposed to cry!"

"Oh, princess, at last I've found you!" said the guard. "We've been under orders from the queen to bring you the news. The king is swiftly dying. He may already be gone. Here, princess. Take my horse. I shall return on foot. I pray you are not too late."

Alzena got on the horse and sped back to the castle. Once there, she left the horse by the kitchen. The cooks saw her running. One of them yelled, "You have to hurry, you don't have much time!"

Running through the corridor, she found her mother standing there with tears pouring down her face.

"Alzena, you've returned in time!"

She ran over to her mother and hugged her fiercely. "Mother, I would travel any distance to be here. Please, take me to him. Let's hurry."

Alzena and Queen Lydia hurried off together for the king's chambers.

Alzena knelt down beside her father's bed. His face gray and sunken, King Pajari slowly opened his eyes. They tracked through the room until they fell on her face, and then happiness and recognition lit up his eyes, followed by sorrow.

"Oh my daughter, I am so sorry for what I did to you in a moment of rage.

How can you forgive a foolish old man?"

Alzena answered, "Please, Father, don't talk now. All is forgiven. I'm back, Father."

A dark shadow hovered in the corner of the room, behind Alzena. Only King Pajari saw it, for she was invisible to everyone else. The voice whispered, "Now your daughter is mine!" and he heard an awful laugh.

King Pajari stared in horror. "My daughter, beware!" he whispered hoarsely.

Alzena touched his hand gently. "Father, what are you saying?"

He answered, "Beware the spirit—she means to enslave you!" King Pajari gasped for breath and his lips lost their color.

"Father?" Alzena cried. "No, Father! It's all right. I forgive you for all you've done to me."

King Pajari moaned, "Beware! Beware! Beware!" His voice quieted with each word. As his heart slowed and stopped, his face was a mask of fear incarnate. King Pajari drew out his last breath with a shuddering groan. The life went out of his eyes, and they stared, motionless, wide with horror at something only he could see.

"No! Father! Father!" Alzena broke into sobs, confused and grieving. She kept holding his hand, even though it was turning cooler and cooler by the second.

"Now he's gone!" cried Alzena. She still couldn't process it.

Alzena turned to Queen Lydia. "Tell me what happened. What took Pajari away?" she asked.

"You have seen as clearly as me that your father has not been himself. He would do horrible things, ordering the servants around and slapping them. He almost killed a guard just for taking a break after working all night. The guard had my permission. And as he was about to kill the guard, your father clutched his heart and collapsed. We brought him here and now he is gone."

They both hugged each other and cried. Lydia cried for her husband, but Alzena felt a deep void inside, as if she had lost more than her father, but her hope as well.

Alzena eventually went back to her bedroom, because the men were coming in to bear the body to its rightful place and she couldn't stand to see him moved. She grieved for Cato being gone and now her father as well. The sadness drove her into sleep faster than she could prepare.

Alzena realized soon that she was dreaming. There was almost no light in her dream. A thin window far away provided the only illumination. She felt the stones under her bare feet and shrank from the cold. She couldn't get her feet off the floor and felt chains around her legs and scratchy wood underneath her arms, also chained. Her body writhed as she tried to escape the chains around her.

"Let me out!" she tried to scream, but her mouth was covered and only muffled grunts escaped her. She felt something slimy crawling across one of her feet and she tried not to lose her mind with fear as she discovered couldn't even move her foot to shake it off.

"Now you know how it feels, princess. I've been trapped here in this hell for hundreds of years. And now you're going to help me get out!"

"No... No..." Alzena tried to say.

"I want Cato to die! I don't want him to lift the curse. No one was ever supposed to lift the curse. He is ruining all of my plans! And you're going to stop him, because if you don't, I will unleash my dreaded beasts! And this time, I won't stop until every single human in your kingdom is dead! Everyone will pay! This will be my kingdom again! So what's it going to be—the kingdom or your one true love?"

She tried even harder to escape, pushing against the chains and straining in panic.

As the awful voice faded from her mind, she heard, "Choose wisely, princess." Each word sounded farther away.

Chapter Eighteen

The Departure of Alzena

Alzena woke up in a cold sweat, panting in fear. Then she heard the knocking on the door and got up to answer it. Margaret was standing there, still crying. "Alzena, the funeral is beginning soon. Everybody is in mourning. Oh, what a sad day."

"I will be getting ready very soon," answered Alzena. Once the door was closed, she punched the pillow over and over again, screaming.

The funeral ceremony was attended by thousands of people from the local farms, the people from the castle, and from many of the surrounding areas as well. The church pastori, dressed all in black for the somber occasion, was an older man in his 60s. His face was even more somber than the faces in the crowd around him.

All around were over two hundred tombstones, a massive cemetery where all the royal bodies were buried. The kings all were entombed in a great sepulcher in the middle of the cemetery, where the service was held. "Today we lose a great father, a great leader, a great king," said the pastori.

As Alzena listened, she felt a comforting hand on her shoulder. "I've known Cato my whole life. He won't stop for anything to help the people he loves. It may be too late for your father, but it won't be too late for us."

She recognized Kainuu's voice immediately and was proud that he'd dared to come to the funeral. "Thank you, Kainuu," she said.

As the pastori bowed his head, the rest of the people did as well and prayed solemn prayers for the passing of the king. After the prayers were concluded, the pallbearers came up the hill with the coffin. It was so heavy it took three strong soldiers on each side to hold it in the air. Blue and red jewels were embedded in the side of the casket, and the inside was lined with velvet. As they lowered the coffin to a granite slab, the assembled people could see King Pajari inside, dressed in shining armor.

One by one, the people of the kingdom filed by King Pajari, leaving gifts in honor.

Alzena found herself back in the palace after the funeral, talking to Margaret some more. It was like waking up, but she couldn't remember falling asleep. "What did you say, Margaret?"

Margaret asked her again, patiently. "There was something you mentioned earlier this morning. What was it?"

A memory of an old lion speaking to her in a hut came to her mind.

"Yes. Exactly. Margaret, we need to talk about something. When you sent me to Masala's Village, the chief there said they remembered you. Is it true that you used to live there yourself?"

"I did, long before I came here to care for the royal family," said Margaret.

"Why didn't you tell me?" asked Alzena.

"I was so happy to be working for your mother I never thought to tell you of my past. I'm sorry. My parents were farmers, and they were so poor they couldn't feed me anymore. I discovered years later that they had left me in the Forbidden Forest to fend for myself because they thought I was going to starve anyway. But one of their people found me and took me to the village, and I was finally treated with kindness and compassion. They took care of me until I became an adult. Eventually, I came here and found my way into the castle, working as a seamstress for your mother. She was so kind to me. And the day you were born, it was my greatest joy to be your nanny. I have seen the love you have for your people. It is even greater than the love your mother and I share for you. Let that love for your people give you strength."

Alzena started crying again with happiness, but she also remembered what the voice had told her in that nightmare. "There has to be something more than your father's death that's bothering you," said Margaret. "The tears still fall from your eyes, and you're breathing way too fast."

"I've met the Lion-People and the people in Masala's village now," said Alzena. "They are nothing like the stories at all. I have fallen in love with one of them. He is out journeying far on a quest to try and save my father, but now it's too late." She wiped her tears, and her eyes opened wide as the truth dawned on her. "I know what I have to do, Margaret. I love you too. I have to go now."

"Wait!" cried Margaret. "You can't run off like that again! Santara needs you!"

She went downstairs into the royal armory where many suits of armor stood on poles. A gold breastplate with the Goddess of Light imprinted on the front would protect her well. But first, a strong silk mesh went on underneath everything else to protect her from sword strikes. The breastplate went over the mesh. Then she chose a sturdy pair of gauntlets and leg guards.

Her arms were strong, so she pulled a heavy sword and sheath from the wall, swung the sword a few times until she was used to the weight, and returned it to the sheath, hanging it from the side of her armor where she could easily reach it when the need arose. She chose not to wear a helmet because she didn't care who saw her leave anymore.

Fully prepared now, she mounted her horse as if the armor weighed nothing and began to leave the castle. As she was about to cross the drawbridge, her mother saw her. "Alzena, where are you going? Don't do anything rash!" she cried.

"I'm going to do what I have to do, Mother!" she cried loudly from her horse. Then she rode off into the vast open fields, heading back towards the hut where she had left the book. When she arrived at Kainuu's hut, she saw him fishing. "Do you still have the book I left here?" she asked, and he pulled his fishing pole out of the water.

"Exactly where you left it," answered Kainuu. He went and retrieved the book for her. "Your Majesty, where are you going?"

"I'm going to go save him. There's got to be a way!"

"Can I come with you? Can I help?" asked Kainuu.

"No, I'm sorry," she said, putting the book inside her saddlebag. "What I am going to do, I have to do alone." Then she mounted her horse and took off across the fields, looking for Cato. "I'm going to find a way to save the love of my life and the love of my people. I know you are wicked and wise, but I will not let you win!" As she rode out, she brandished her sword against the invisible sorceress, trying to drive the woman out of her mind, and trying to block out everything else but her love for Cato.

Chapter Nineteen

Cato's Journey

The summer sun shone down on Cato the next afternoon. As his horse carried him through a vast field of grasses and grains, he wished for the coolness of the trees and the healing waters of the forest.

Cato watched the grassland roll by beneath the horse's hooves, and he noticed shadows on the ground. He looked up and saw trees towering above his head, not like the ones in the Forbidden Forest, but more alive and growing, happy and green in the bright sun, not choking each other out.

He sensed a good place to rest nearby, and as the trees surrounded him with their coolness, he heard the splashing of water and knew he was near a river.

The river appeared through the trees, and the horse stopped by the water. Cato dropped from the horse, trying to find a good hiding place nearby as he crept along the ground to get to the water's edge. He saw many bushes where he could hide. He reached the water's edge and dropped his head into the flow, desperately sucking in liquid as fast as he could, for he was very thirsty after a full day of riding. His horse also drank greedily beside him.

After relieving his great thirst, he lifted his head and looked around. He heard a woman screaming. Two men from the forest were attacking her by the shore, leaving the trees in their violence. Even though he was tired, he found the strength to get up and yell. The men fled as soon as they saw him. Soon, shouts from other men came. By the time the bowmen emerged from the forest, all they could see was Cato and the woman.

The bowmen began shooting arrows at Cato, and he ran as fast as he could through the bushes back to his horse.

He leaped up on the horse's back and they crossed the river, but not fast enough.

As they crossed the river, one of the bowmen's arrows sailed right through the air and into Cato's shoulder. He roared in pain and shock and urged the horse faster. As they disappeared into the trees, the bowmen kept firing, but stopped when he was out of range.

Cato kept moving quickly through the forest, towards the base of the volcano.

When he reached the meadows, he became aware of a cave on one side. He knew it would be a perfect place to hide. The sun was setting again, and it was time for his nightly agony.

As he got inside the cave, he drew the arrow out of his skin and screamed in pain as the flesh tore from the barbed tip. As the light dimmed, Cato hid and waited for the change, his muscles in agony from the poison in the arrow. As he turned into a lion, the pain was even greater than usual. He emerged from the cave into the dark of night, gasping.

"The poison!" he grunted. "I must find goldenseal soon!" Cato searched through the meadow, his strong lion nose detecting flowers from miles away.

The scent of goldenseal was only a hundred feet away, though. Crawling through the grass, Cato found the tiny yellow flowers in a grove of trees. He smashed them with his paws to break them open and then bit a big leaf from a nearby bush and used it to get the paste onto his shoulder. The poison was coursing through his body, leaving nasty purple veins and a deep mark where the arrow had entered at the center.

Within a few seconds, the wound had stopped swelling and the purple veins had shrunk back beneath the skin. Soon, he was able to breathe deeply again.

Cato traveled through the forest by night, blending in with the pale grass and unseen as he padded along on all fours, silent beneath the din of the crickets. All of a sudden, he smelled another flower he was looking for. He hadn't smelled it since the medicine man had shown it to him. Since it only bloomed this week of the year, he hurried over to where the honey scent beckoned him to ravensblood, a dark red flower that would only expose its smell in the light of the full moons.

Cato ran back with many of these flowers in his jaws.

As he kept looking for the other flowers, he became more frustrated. He had to travel far into the forest to locate the forsythias, but eventually, he found them. He followed their smell to a small lake in the forest, where they grew all around the shore. He slashed through the stems of several stalks and made the long journey back to the base of the mountain, where he dropped the forsythia flowers by the ravensblood.

Having smelled no chrysanthemums the way he had traveled before, he went in the other direction through the forest. Eventually, he found a place where zinnias and marigold and sunflowers bloomed. However, their scents could not hide the delicate sea-breeze smell of the precious chrysanthemums with their majestic purple blooms. He got several of these and returned to the horse.

Once he had slept and rested for the night, the morning sun woke him by his transformation back to a human. He roared in pain, but resisted the urge to keep crying out because he knew he needed to save his energy for the long climb up the volcano ahead.

He took the rope from the horse, wrapped the bundle of flowers, and tied it around his back to keep them safe. The horse wandered free, not interested in Cato's choice to ascend the mountain.

Chapter Twenty

The Volcano

The meadow sloped upward, and above the meadow, endless waves of rocks until the top of the volcano far above. A red glow behind the black rocks suggested lava inside.

He shouldered his burdens more securely and began the ascent. As the gravel underneath his feet became steeper and steeper, he began to slip and fall back. Cato mustered his courage and pressed on. High above him, he saw the walls of jagged stones like a maze. As he studied the pathways, he lost his footing again and slipped, hitting his shoulder as he fell.

Cato dug his legs into the gravel and stopped himself, then continued on up the mountain, massaging his shoulder to stop the pain. Once he reached the maze of boulders, he found himself more confused. He kept trying to go uphill, but many times the pathways forced him back down, away from his goal. He found one particularly large boulder rising far above the others, and racing to the top, tried to get a better view to fix it in his mind.

The trail from this viewpoint was obvious. There were only a few more turns and he would be clear of the field of boulders. Above that, the journey would only become rockier and steeper, although he would be clear of the strange jagged boulders that had blocked his path for hours. However, he saw that it was still a great distance to the top, and that the sun was falling towards the land already.

He went back down the slope, and no longer lost, was confidently able to get himself out of the maze before the sun completely set. As night fell, he was grateful for the change.

For once it was a blessing, not a burden. After he had become a powerful lion with sharp claws, it was much easier to find purchase on the rocks, and the pads on his toes made the journey less painful by grabbing the edges of the rock without being punctured.

Deep into the night he climbed, the stars and the two moons lighting his way very brightly. He looked up and wondered at how much closer they looked, so far up the volcano. As the moons shone brightly above him and wandered on their nightly trek to the horizon, he realized that day was about to dawn.

Although he kept his eyes on the rocks as he climbed, he could not help glancing around as the sky went from black to deep blue to purple. As dawn approached, he watched as a whole rainbow of colors exploded from the sky and the magnificent sun rose into the air.

He stopped and prepared for the return to humanity. As he changed, he felt the pain, but at the same time, he felt the triumph as he realized he was very near the peak. The air glowed red above from the lava boiling inside. Once a human, Cato was able to untie to rope and find the flowers. He put them together like he had been told by Alzena and the ravensblood flowers began to glow, powered, he imagined, by the light of the sun, forming a beam of light that Alzena promised would show him the way. He pointed the flower at the peak, and its light played across the surface. Suddenly, the light disappeared into a cave on the slopes. Cato hurried towards it, but he was interrupted by a horrific shriek. He turned around.

A firebird, still blazing from the lava and furious at its territory being invaded, swooped towards Cato. Its talons were large enough that he had to duck to avoid being ripped apart. As it swayed through the air, screeching in rage at missing, Cato ran as fast as he could up the side of the volcano, forgetting the pain in his legs, and got into the cave before the bird could circle back. He noticed rocks hanging precariously from the roof, and that gave him an idea.

With all of his strength he leaped, yelling, and pounded two clumps of loose rocks with all his might. As they hit the ground, it began a cascading earthquake that sent hundreds of rocks down around him. As he raced inside, dodging the boulders, he saw the exit fill with stones and the satisfying thump as the firebird crashed into them, unable to follow him. Beaten, the firebird screamed loudly, and was heard no more.

Cato rolled to safety in a round area where nothing was falling, collected himself and his precious bundle of flowers, and continued deeper into the cave, led forward by glowing orange light from the lava below him, shining through the floor and filling the cavern like he was inside the setting sun. He went deeper.

Chapter Twenty-One

The Fire Goddess

Cato found himself walking along pathways of dried lava. As he looked through a crack in the floor, he realized he was standing on a thin volcanic shelf as he could see the chamber and the lava below. He took a moment to peer inside.

He had seen many lakes made of water before, but never one made of pure fire, fire that bubbled and cracked and spat big red bubbles into the air. The deep chamber percolated with fury.

He pulled himself back up, mesmerized, and continued deeper into the cave. He found a chamber that was lit by candles. The ceiling rose high, like a funnel sucking hot air out of the cavern to blow across his face.

A pool of fresh lava bubbled on the floor. It was from there that he saw a body emerge, a woman, skin burned from the fire eternally encircling her. Her four arms blazed, two on each side, and in her flinty face her eyes shone blood red like two rubies hardened by the pressure of the lava.

"You will look upon me!" cried the woman of fire.

Cato, having looked away in fear, brought his eyes to meet her stern gaze. Once they locked eyes, Uta stared deeply into him, and he felt her gaze burning all the way down to his soul. It was like having someone read your mind, someone dangerous and scary that could hurt you if they knew what you were thinking.

After staring at Cato with a deep concentration, she declared what she had seen.

"You! You have been removed of your humanity! You and your people have been doomed by this curse."

Cato hung his head, terrified to meet her gaze, astonished at how quickly she had read his mind.

"But you astonish me, monster!"

Cato lifted his head back up, amazed.

"None of your kind, not one of the Lion-People, has ever dared to reach this place before! Tell me, mortal, what do you hope to get from me?"

Cato responded with what he had always dreamed of. "As has been written, I am here to restore my lost humanity. I am here to redeem my stolen heart. I am here to free my creature-ridden soul. That is what I hope to get from you."

Uta laughed scornfully, and Cato cringed.

"Foolish creature. That is what you dream of. That power lies within you alone. For me to give you access to that power, you have to prove to me that you are willing to separate the human from the beast and overcome its wild, animal power."

"What do I have to do?" he asked, now unsure of the task ahead of him. How many more surprises did Uta have in store for him?

"If you can defeat that fire demon, the one that torments us from the volcano, it will open the way to his altar, where he guards our most sacred chalice."

Cato was uncomfortable at the thought of open battle after the long journey to the peak of the volcano. He thought about Alzena and his people and discovered he still had the strength he needed. He noticed a glowing passageway behind Uta as a deep rumbling emerged.

Emboldened, he asked, "Who is the fire demon?"

Uta said, "The fire demon Palo possesses the Chalice of Plenty. Its theft has caused an endless thirst in the throats of mankind. No matter how much ale he quaffs, no matter how much water he swallows, man cannot slake his thirst. Unless you can help, mankind will become thirstier and thirstier, even at their mother's breast. Your task will not be easy. Many have tried to defeat Palo, and many have fallen to a fiery death."

"I believe I can master this challenge," answered Cato. "My human heart is pure, full of love for one woman. Still, the heart of the beast inside me is restless, angry, tired. But with both of my hearts, my will, and my love, I will do whatever it takes to lift this curse. Even sacrifice my own life if I have to. As it is written." Cato's voice began to break with emotion, but he fought against the tears to finish his message. "My people have to be free of this curse. I promise you that this monster will be slain. Tell me, do you know how to defeat this demon?"

Uta answered, "I will show you something that might be useful to you."

She produced a magical, glowing weapon in the air and gave it to Cato. It looked like a normal sword, about two feet long, but even as she held it the weapon seemed to come alive at her touch, humming with power. "This great weapon is known as Jumala, or 'The Will of the Gods.' Whatever weapon you desire in your mind and your heart, that's what it will become. Whatever you need— ice, fire, wind, sword, bow and arrow, spear, or axe, it shall be yours."

"I shall be strong, Goddess. I will prevail." He held it and instantly felt the energy connect with him, tasting his mind and then settling in his hands, ready to use.

She pointed to the passage. "Beyond this wall lies Palo's lair. Defeat him and you will return peace to this turbulent volcano."

Cato walked inside the cavern with his weapon. Sweat began to collect on his face from the heat. He felt that ice would be best for defeating a fire demon, but he grappled with the question of what kind of weapon to use. Hot acrid air forced its way into his throat and he gagged, covering his face with his clothing to protect himself. As he got closer, hot embers began to fly through the air, stinging his skin as they flew past him.

Bravely forcing his way through the hot wind, Cato turned the corner and found himself in the main chamber. The volcano had built many layers through time, but at the heart was a glowing crater full of boiling lava, more than he had ever conceived of.

Across the deep crater, a long, precarious stone platform led to the other side, where a great demon stood. He struggled to see clearly through the heat-waves, but could tell Palo was massive. He towered over the altar, much taller than Cato, and his muscles bulged with unnatural power. His armor sparkled with flames. His eyes were two glowing embers in his face.

He brandished a huge longsword made of rainbow-colored spectrolite. Cato saw the blade as a further insult to the Goddess of Light that he had worshipped his whole life.

As he stood there, his very presence threatening and his sword held at the ready, Palo roared across the crater.

"Foolish mortal, you have one chance, and only one, to turn around and leave. *Now!*"

Cato waited several strategic seconds before responding, and then roared back across the pit, "I did not come all this way just to be turned back by something like you."

His great wings flapping, Palo surged across the stones, roaring. He was approaching with terrible speed and Cato knew he had to act quickly. He turned to the weapon in his hands and knew exactly what he needed. "Ice arrows and bow!" he cried, and focused with all of his might.

Cato felt the energy shift in the weapon and in his mind, and before his eyes, the weapon transformed into a strong bow already loaded with a freezing cold ice arrow. He pulled the string back and tried to aim the weapon. It was difficult to gauge exactly where to loose the arrow because Palo was moving fast and the heat was distorting his vision and distracting him, but he focused with great strength and released the arrow, feeling the sting as the ice flew past his cheek.

Palo saw what Cato had done and swung his sword to deflect the arrow, sending it falling into the lava below. As the arrow hit the blade, shockwaves of ice flew down the sword and onto Palo's arms. He roared in pain and landed on the stone pathway for a second. But he only stopped to catch his breath. "You'll have to do better than that, mortal!" he cried from the bridge.

Before Palo could take off running and flying, Cato had already readied another arrow and managed to fire. Palo moved forward, but not quite fast enough and it sliced directly through his fiery wing.

The wing froze solid and broke into hundreds of shards of ice. Palo screamed in pain and fell to the stones again as pieces of ice fell down and were vaporized in the heat of the volcano, sizzling and steaming as they disappeared.

Palo tried to fly again, but with only one wing, was earthbound. He began to move on foot across the stone, roaring in fury as he came. As he made the final distance, Cato had time for another arrow. Palo deflected it with his sword, but was visibly shaken as the ice chips enshrouded his body and he was slowed down considerably. He strode directly before Cato and swung his sword overhead towards him.

Cato rolled out of the way as the sword came down with a thundering crash into the rock where he'd been standing. He rolled to his knees and readied another arrow, turning. Palo raised his sword high above his head, preparing for the kill. He glared viciously.

"Die, mortal!" he roared.

That extra second made all the difference in the world. Cato took advantage of that instant and let his arrow fly. It flew through the air for an instant and buried itself deep inside Palo's unguarded chest. Palo screamed in agony, but his scream was cut off by a strange crackling sound that emerged from his throat as if his vocal cords had suddenly turned to ice. Palo stood strangely still. Within seconds, ice began to spread from his chest across his entire body. The crackling ice covered every inch of his body like a gown and froze him to the very spot.

Cato got to his feet and went over to where the frozen fire demon stood, eyes gaping wide in shock and still full of red life. With a deep, victorious roar, Cato swung his fists at the fire demon. In a sparkling crash, Palo shattered into hundreds of pieces and the ice crystals fell to the floor, already melting from the heat of the volcano and sending puffs of steam into the hot air.

Finally free to cross the bridge to the altar, Cato boldly walked it. Many treasures waited on the other side, but Cato only wanted one. On the altar before him stood the Chalice of Plenty, even in the demon's eyes deserving a special place by itself. The Chalice was covered in precious jewels of many different colors. It shone brilliantly in the light, and as Cato picked it up, he knew that his first task was complete. With newfound vigor, already feeling renewed, Cato hurried out of the volcanic crater and back to Uta.

He presented the sacred Chalice to Uta, beaming with pride at his accomplishment.

"Excellent, Cato. You care more for other mortals than you care for your own life. Alzena was right to send you to me."

Cato stared at Uta in surprise. "How did you know about Alzena?"

Uta smiled knowingly. "The Chalice you have found is the first step. The next step is to fill it with the Sacred Water. Wrap the Chalice well and guard it, for you have to bring it to the land of the Ice Goddess."

Cato asked, "And where is that?"

Uta said, "At the edge of the sea, you will find a great ice cavern. It hides the Temple of Ice. There, my sister, Kide, the Goddess of Ice, will be waiting for you." She pointed to another door, where Cato saw the open sky. "Down the other side of this volcano, where many forests grow, is your destination. A small trail will lead you safely to the trees. Keep going until you reach the ocean. Kide is waiting."

Cato walked out of the cavern, blinking in the bright light.

As he exited the cave, he looked up and thought of Alzena. "One down, my love. That's two to go!"

Chapter Twenty-Two

The Goddess of Ice

Cato looked down the far side of the volcano. Rainclouds hung from the slopes, and not far below, he saw the beginning of a rainforest that grew all the way down to the ocean where a splinter of a beach in the distance hugged the trees and the vast water.

As he descended the trail, he found it was much easier going down than up, because gravity was agreeing with him. He went towards the trees until he reached the grass and tiny shrubs that marked the beginning of the forest. He walked much easier then, through grass that gave way to trees that were shorter than he was, and finally through a dense rainforest where pine trees absorbed most of the water but left an abundance for the flowers and ferns of the forest floor. As he strode, always downhill, through this wild, untouched landscape, he couldn't help but notice the magnificent beauty around him. It seemed so much more peaceful and abundant than the Forbidden Forest he grew up in.

After what seemed like at least two hours traveling through trees, he finally broke out and found himself before the endless ocean, stretching out into an unbroken blue line of horizon. The smell of the ocean, salty and tangy, was something completely new to him. The sky was blazing so bright with the light of the sun and a huge flaming reflection bounced off the waves. Cato had to shield his eyes with his hand because it was far too bright.

As he closed his eyes, the smell of the ocean became even stronger, and the cacophony of seagulls began to outweigh the pounding in his ears from the long journey down the mountain.

Cato walked along the jagged rocks and pebbles that made up the long coastline and looked into the chaotic, booming surf. Away out to sea, Cato witnessed whales coming to the surface and sounding, exhaling steaming air out of their blowholes in spurts that could be seen from shore.

Although he was entranced by the unmatched view, he turned around to witness an even stranger sight. The mouth of a gigantic ice cavern loomed behind him. Somehow, despite the warmth of the sun, this glacier had made its way down to the sea and refused to melt. A river had carved a cavern out inside the glacier. Knowing this was his destination, Cato approached the cave, trying to navigate the treacherous jagged rocks and crusty ocean life in the tide pools scattered along the beach.

As he reached the cavern, he noticed that there were flashes of light reflecting off the ice-blue ceiling. Each flash was bouncing off a facet of the cavern's scalloped roof, which was ever so slowly melting and dripping into the river that flowed beside him.

As he got deeper into the cave, following the flickers of light and the freezing cold river, Cato had to adjust to the darkness, although filtered blue light still oozed through the ceiling. Around a bend in the river and the cave, Cato made his way to a large cavern where a bright yellow candle burned on an altar, beckoning. In this large chamber, the ice had remained in places, holding the ceiling up with crystal pillars. The roof shone gold from the candle, blue from the river, and purple from another body of water flowing off in another direction.

As he approached Kide, he wondered if she herself was frozen, because at first he didn't see her move as he approached. Her clothing was translucent and all he saw was her face. The back of the cave seemed copied in her dress. Behind her dress, he noticed her waves of shimmering white hair, like a waterfall down her smooth back, which he had at first mistaken for ice. Then she began to move to the side, and nearer, and he saw that her body was translucent, like water. In contrast, her eyes were ice blue. They were piercing pools of color that glowed with their own power from a face that he couldn't read any emotion from.

Kide stood taller than Cato and looked down at him. Like Uta, she stared into his eyes before speaking.

"Cato," said the Goddess of Ice. "My sister told me you were coming. You are so brave to make it this far. May I see the Chalice of Plenty?"

Cato unwrapped the sacred Chalice and carried it over to her waiting hands.

"It's been away from my hands for centuries," said Kide. "My grandfather once held this Chalice as well. Just touching it restores my spirit. You must take good care of it, for you need to fill the Chalice of Plenty with the Sacred Water."

Cato received the Chalice and wrapped it up carefully as she continued.

"Not just any water will do. The Water of Hope is what you need. To drink from that water, you have to travel deep beneath the waves, but only after defeating the guardian, Monodon. There is a pearl, a black pearl, deep inside his tusk. You need this pearl to open the way to the Sacred Water."

"This sounds like a daunting task," said Cato. "A great battle, traveling underwater, and a dark pearl? Is there anything you can give me to help me in this quest, dear lady?"

"My seahorse Autta should be able to help you. He can help you breathe underwater, he can help you fight, and he knows every inch of these waters."

She whistled a beautiful tune that rang through the ice cavern like it was an amphitheater, and Cato was amazed at the resonance. The sound of the ancient melody was calming, and for the first time since entering, he felt warm.

Then he saw the dark blue water that went the other way towards the ocean, and a surging, foaming tail dashing through it. Then the seahorse, Autta, swam up and pushed himself above the water, displaying his incredible features. The seahorse was every color of the rainbow, and was obviously important to Kide, for he was graced with a gold saddle and the finest reins for him to grab hold of.

"Thank you for helping me," he said, nodding to Autta as well. Autta stood taller with happiness. "I shall do as you ask. But tell me, where is this Monodon?"

"You shall find it in the Blue Lagoon, where this water empties into," she said, pointing to the blue waterway. "From here, though, you will need to breathe like a fish."

"But I was not made for breathing underwater. I was born with the power to run through the forest, invisible."

"I have a helmet that will let you breathe underwater, and my seahorse is not just your guide, but your guardian. He will not let anything happen to you."

Cato thought he saw the seahorse smiling with pride at Kide, but he was not sure if it could really do that. However, he had never seen a seahorse as big as a human before either, although tiny ones had occasionally swum upriver into the Forbidden Forest, where he had watched them with wonder until they were eaten by carp or trout. He was glad that this seahorse was much stronger and bigger.

Cato put on his helmet, which covered his entire face and pulled tight around his neck with a cord, and found that he could breathe quite well. He entered the water, gasping at the cold. Even completely submerged, the mask continued delivering fresh air, filtering it from the water in some way that he couldn't divine. He grabbed the reins attached to Autta, and Autta began swimming, fast enough to pull him underwater as he was dragged behind through the cold water. He watched as schools of multicolored fish swam nearby, going up and down the river on their own business. As he turned to look above, he saw the sun shining through the water and knew he was free of the cave.

As Cato entered the lagoon, the water became much deeper and an underwater universe welcomed him. He let go of Autta's reins and floated in the water, looking around. Many fish swam here, but they all stayed away from a large shadow he could see at the bottom of the lagoon. Through the waves he could see Monodon's purple bulk and its long dark tusk. He was pretty sure that it saw him. He swam to where he could rest his feet in the sand, brought his head above water, and looked around his surroundings to prepare for battle.

Cato was on the edge of a lagoon hundreds of feet across and deep enough to turn the water a dark blue. Autta was still right by his side, ready to protect him from Monodon if the need arose. Around him were shores with very fine sand, and rocks providing a natural barricade from the ocean. Cato saw Monodon rising to the surface, and he held his weapon at the ready. "Weapon, heed my will and heart! I need the strongest steel, the sword of the Goddess of Light!"

In a magic shimmer, the weapon became the strongest sword ever forged. Monodon broke the surface and screamed. It was over twenty feet long, four or five times taller than Cato. But in front of that massive dark purple body, the narwhal had a single light brown spike that ran straight out of its head for more than half that length. Swooping up and down and using its powerful body to lunge through the water, Monodon took a lunging swing at Cato.

Cato dodged and swung his sword, but Monodon was faster. The horn raked across his arm, slicing it, and Cato dropped the sword, moaning in pain. He fell into the water. It became murky around him as blood poured out of his arm. He saw his sword lying on the sandy floor of the lagoon beneath him. Panicking, he swung himself around in the water and reached as far as he could. As he finally reached far enough to grab the sword in his hand securely, he felt a rush of bubbles and the thump of the saddle between his legs.

Autta lunged above the water, giving Cato an advantage. Monodon chased after him fiercely, jabbing his horn every chance he got and screaming loudly. Cato turned backwards and began answering his jabs with swings of his own, successfully blocking his attacks now that he knew the way it lunged.

As his blade connected with the horn repeatedly, it sent shockwaves down into the body of the narwhal, and it screamed louder. Small chunks of the horn fell into the water, and black blood dripped behind it.

The narwhal chased Autta and Cato around the lagoon, but Autta had a better idea, being more agile than the bulky narwhal. He reared up suddenly out of the water, kicking violently, and as he rose into the air, he spun backwards.

Monodon surged out of the water behind him, furious at the new tactic. As Cato hung upside down for a second over Monodon, he saw his chance.

As Monodon rose, its gigantic body caused it to slow down quickly. As the great beast slowed, it bucked forward, and Cato pushed himself down off of Autta, building up greater speed as he fell.

He held the sword tightly in both hands and as he plunged down, he swung the sword as hard as he could through the base of Monodon's tusk. The entire tusk cleaved clean away from the body. Only a trace remained attached, leaking dark blood.

Releasing its final, agonized screams, Monodon sank beneath the surface of the lagoon and disappeared from sight.

Cato dragged the heavy tusk out of the water, using the last of his energy to haul it ashore. He removed his helmet because the battle was over. Autta remained in the water and watched him carefully.

As Cato reached the shore, exhausted and bleeding, he saw seaweed lying on the sand. He reached into a pouch he carried the goldenseal in. He put the goldenseal paste on the seaweed and used it as a salve for his wound.

After several seconds, the bleeding stopped, for the most part, enough for him to focus on the work ahead of him. Cato stared into the hollow end of the tusk, where he had cut it off Monodon. He could see a black round stone wedged inside.

"The black pearl!" cried Cato in excitement.

Removing it was no easy task. He reached into his pouch and found a small curved knife that he used for woodcarving. He used the end of it to sneak under the pearl and pry it loose. With a little work, it sprung free, and he had to catch it in mid-air as it tried to pop away from him. He put the pearl in his pouch, along with the knife, and closed it tightly to keep the prize safe. Then, completely overcome with exhaustion, Cato fell asleep.

When he awoke, it was because Autta kept splashing around in the water, making so much noise that he opened his eyes to see what was going on with him. Feeling better, Cato got up and looked around.

The seahorse kept swimming over to the rocks between the lagoon and the ocean and jumping, but Cato could see that he needed help to reach the ocean. He went over to the seahorse and helped carry him over the rocks, even though he was large.

After he got the seahorse into the waiting ocean, he swam merrily around and came back to shore, looking at Cato. Cato remembered from Kide's instructions that he was supposed to follow Autta to the Water of Hope. Autta waited as Cato went back to the lagoon to put on his helmet and secured it, then returned to the ocean and entered the waves where Autta waited.

He grabbed hold of the reins and the seahorse surged through the water again, quickly submerging and going deep underwater. Even with the air-giving helmet, Cato felt dizzy as they went deeper and deeper. He felt the pressure on his bones increase as he sank.

The ocean floor dropped away swiftly, and deep below them, Cato could see a stone temple sunken under the water. A massive stone gate blocked the entrance. As Cato slowly descended, he found himself directly in front of the gate, where there were many black stones.

One small pit in the surface of the gate was empty. Cato removed the pearl from his pouch and placed it carefully in the pit, hearing it slide into place with some ancient locking mechanism.

As the great underwater gate rose out of the way, groaning with the immense strength it took to lift the rocky barrier, the inside of the temple was revealed to him.

Some force Cato could not divine forced the water away from the center of the room. As he crossed the strange barrier, he felt his body tingle, and then he fell into the room, rolling. Now that he was in the air, he removed his helmet so he could drink the water. The air inside the chamber tasted stale and old.

In the center of the room was a fountain with the words "The Water of Hope" inscribed upon it.

Cato carefully removed the Chalice from its pouch and filled it with this pure water, shining green from the copper fountain.

He drank from the Chalice, and as he drank he could feel the beast inside him growing far weaker. Cato got dizzy, and he leaned against the fountain for balance. He could see his reflection in the water. The image of the lion emerged halfway across his face, and slowly disappeared again with a look of severe anguish.

As Cato continued to look at his reflection, he saw his face entirely replaced by a vision of Alzena's smiling face, and it gave him the hope he was looking for. He pushed himself to his feet and shook the dizziness away, but as he walked away to return to Autta, he kept falling to his knees. As he fell for the second time, he grabbed his air helmet and put it back on. As he secured it, he felt less weak as cleaner air poured in.

Autta was waiting for him right outside. He grabbed hold of the reins and pulled himself onto the seahorse. He hung on for dear life, trying not to collapse as the seahorse valiantly struggled to bring him back to the surface. He swam upriver into the Ice Cavern, as Cato took his helmet off and breathed in the pure, sweet air.

It was such a relief after breathing through the helmet for so long. The damp air provided by the helmet was no replacement for fresh air full of delicious smells and warm breezes. His lungs were hungry for air, and he found himself yawning, opening his jaws wide like a lion. He was overwhelmed with joy at his success.

His strength returned to him with every breath.

Kide was waiting for him in the main chamber. She looked at him carefully, as if she saw right through him to the beast within and Alzena's love in his heart.

"Your body has been purified by these trials. The beast inside you has been weakened. But he has not yet been defeated."

"So my quest is not over?"

"Your own quest to free your people from this curse will not be complete until after you meet my sister, the Goddess of Air. She was once known as the Goddess of Light. She is the most powerful goddess alive, more powerful than Uta herself. Only the Goddess of Air has what you need to break the curse forever."

Cato asked, "How do I get to the land of the Goddess of Air? I know of no fish that can fly."

"There are sailfish that do fly, but fish are not all that I command. The blue peacock is also my child. Her thousand eyes watch the ocean without sleeping. After what you have gone through for me, I know I can trust you with my bird, Lintu. Come outside and I will show you."

Cato followed Kide outside the glacier to the rocky beach.

Kide once again whistled a strange song, this one quite different from the one she sang to summon Autta, a series of trills and dips that was heavenly to his ears. A large shadow emerged from the sky, and a giant peacock, her wings over fifty feet long and her back wide enough to hold a saddle for passengers, landed with a gentle tap on the rocks. Her tail was even more impressive than her wings as she spread it and all the eyes were exposed, staring back at him, it seemed.

"With Lintu's help, you can go anywhere you need. Go now, find my sister, and break the curse that has held your people for far too long."

The saddle had ropes that allowed people to scramble up to the saddle. Cato prepared to get on the gigantic bird and leave, but before he could climb up, Kide said, "Before you go, there is one more thing." She took a ceremonial blade she carried around her waist, and cut a piece of her silvery hair. She placed the tuft of icy hair in a small turquoise locket. "For my sister, Valo, the Goddess of Air. She will know. And now the Chalice?"

Cato handed her the Chalice of Plenty.

"Now the people will never thirst again," she said. "Order will be restored. These lands will once again be a sanctuary for humans. Go now, Lintu! Take Cato to the Goddess of Air!"

Cato climbed onto the saddle and gave the back of the bird a gentle slap. She rose into the air, and Cato grabbed the ropes on the side of the saddle, realizing that without them he would fall to the ground.

Chapter Twenty-Three

The Bowmen

Alzena rode through the woods on horseback. No one followed her, and no one blocked her path. As she rode through the woods, she cried out for Cato over and over again, but his roar never answered her. Only the chittering of the squirrels and the mocking of the blue jays answered her cries. As she called out for Cato again and again, her voice got hoarse and raspy, and she was happy when she reached the cool water of the river.

Alzena dismounted at the water's edge and drank freely from the cold water. Refreshed, she looked around. Her horse was still happily drinking. The sweat from the long run stood out on the horse's white spots. She saw that the bowmen were standing nearby, drinking liquor instead of water. Several of the men were swaggering around by the water's edge and skipping stones for fun.

She knew these men were paid by the queen to guard the forest from anything that might come from the volcano, or anything else that would do the king harm. To think that his servants were out here, getting drunk and having a good time instead of protecting the forest! It made her even angrier than she already was. As she watched quietly, two of the men skipping rocks talked to each other.

"You have to shoot the arrow through three trees in a row and still hit the target to win the queen's gold trophy!" he said, skipping a rock far across the river.

Princess Alzena mounted her horse and led it upriver, towards the bowmen. The other bowman looked downriver, and said, "Look, it's the princess!"

The first bowman turned around and said, "Princess!"

The other men who were drinking liquor out of small flasks put them away and began to get to their knees to bow. As everyone bowed before her, Princess

Alzena rode up to them.

All the men spoke at once. "Princess Alzena, Your Majesty, how can we help you?"

She spoke to the one with the flask in his hand first. "Give me that flask! You men are supposed to be serving the queen, not getting drunk!" She grabbed the flask and dumped the rest of the liquor on the ground. "All of you!" The sound of liquor splashing on the ground filled her ears for a few seconds. "I bet you couldn't stand in a straight line if you tried! The time for pleasantries is over now! I am on a very urgent mission! Have any of you seen a man riding through here, a man that may have looked like a lion, a man with golden hair? He is in grave danger! I must find him!"

The leader of the bowmen lifted his head up again. "Your Majesty, we have seen him. Wulff shot him, he's one of our best bowmen!"

"Well, that's not saying much," scoffed Alzena.

"The man of which you speak terrified one of our women," said Wulff, "and we thought she would hurt her, so we had to protect her."

"You dared to injure Cato? I must speak to the man who shot him at once!" As she spoke from her horse, the men kept their eyes down on the white spots on the black horse she rode, avoiding her eyes.

The leader of the bowmen walked over to Wulff, who was looking nervous, and stood right before him.

"Wulff! Come with me!" said the lead bowman.

Wulff said, "Yes, sir!"

The lead bowman kept his hand firmly squeezed to Wulff's shoulder as they approached.

"You!" Alzena cried, and Wulff cringed. "Look at me!" Wulff dared to look at her as her battle armor shone bright in the sun and her red hair flowed like blood from her head, and as he stared at her, he found himself unable to lie to her. "I'm sorry, Your Majesty."

"How dare you shoot Cato? Did you harm him in any way?" she asked, glaring at him.

Wulff was still very scared, but opened his mouth to speak. "Your Majesty, forgive me, but when I shoot, I never miss. The arrow went through his arm by his shoulder. The arrows were poison, Your Majesty. I'm afraid he may not get very far."

Alzena slapped Wulff across the face, and Wulff hung his head in shame. She leaned over and got directly in his face. "I should have your bow for this!" she screamed. "Which way did he go?"

Without looking up, Wulff said, "He and his horse were heading across the river to the Ravensblood Mountain, Your Majesty. That way," he said, pointing across the river.

"Well, at least you're being honest," said Alzena. "You two there, lock him up for now and keep him there until I get back. Then I'll figure out how to deal with him properly."

The two men she had commanded went over to Wulff and took him by the shoulders. As Alzena was heading towards the river, she stopped her horse. She turned around one more time and shouted back, "And if any of you ever see him again, don't you hurt a hair on his head, or I'm going to punish you even worse than what's coming to Wulff!"

Alzena crossed the river, and started seeing spots of blood in the forest. She followed the trail. As she went deeper, she found the meadow where Cato had searched for the healing flowers. Dried blood was all over the place.

"No! Cato!" Alzena cried out in horror.

As Alzena sat there on her horse, sobbing, she heard the Evil Sorceress inside her mind.

"Cato is dead," she whispered gleefully. *"Your mother's own bowmen killed him, Princess!"*

Alzena looked around, trying to see the Evil Sorceress. Her dark shadow was well hidden in the trees. "No! No! It's not true! Don't say that! I hate you! I know you're just trying to trick me, like you tricked my father, like you tricked so many people, but you're not going to trick me! My love for Cato and my love for my good people will overwhelm your evil and your hatred!"

As Alzena sat there and drew in a deep breath, she felt a cool breeze on her face, and she felt as light as a feather as the burden was lifted from her mind and her shoulders. She breathed deeply, believing she had escaped the torment of the Evil Sorceress, and continued through the forest.

Alzena entered the meadow at the base of the mountain, seeing the cave. Finding Cato's blood inside, she knew that he had come this way.

She made a fire by the entrance to the cave, and in the light of the fire, she carefully read every page of the old book, searching for any clues on how to destroy the Evil Sorceress.

Alzena read many things about strange creatures and even stranger goddesses, and sometimes gods as well, and spells and magic and strange words that she couldn't even begin to decipher.

Nothing in the book told her anything about defeating the Evil Sorceress, and as she finished the book, she thumped it down to the cave floor by the fire, discouraged and tired.

Sleep overtook her.

Suddenly, she snapped her eyes open, jolted awake by the cold stone floor underneath her feet.

She was in another nightmare, chained to a chair again and unable to move. She fought against the chains with all her might, but was still unable to escape. As she struggled, she heard the evil voice inside her mind again.

Whispering, she said, *"Did you really think you could defeat me? You? You're going to have to try harder than that, child! You have failed, Princess! I will kill your love, and I will kill your people as well! You can never stop me!"*

Alzena fought harder, even though the voice was already inside her mind and her heart was racing in fear, sending cold ice through her veins.

"No! Stop! Stop! Please! Please, stop! No! No! Stop it! Leave me alone!"

Alzena felt herself getting weaker and weaker and slowly losing control.

Chapter Twenty-Four

The Goddess of Air

Cato flew higher and higher on Lintu's back. The great peacock swooped in large circles, her extremely long wings flapping ponderously as they rose, in ever-climbing arcs, through the sky above the ocean.

As they rose higher, Cato saw clouds around him, and the volcano was getting to be below him, and even the puffy clouds were getting smaller. As they rose, the volcano and the land looked like a tiny speck on the edge of the ocean. Above him, he craned his neck to see another higher cloud bank, like a white ceiling in the heavens.

As they passed through these clouds, Cato was surprised to discover they were just far away rain. Rising above the misty bank, Cato was amazed at the unfiltered light of the sun, and the reflections off the white clouds were astoundingly bright. Cato was close to the top of the sky, and the stars shone through the thin air.

Above the puffy layer of clouds were big islands floating through the air, and on the largest of them was a grand palace of shining crystal, reflecting the blue and orange of the majestic sky-scape and the white puffs of clouds below.

The great peacock landed on the ground before the palace. On this island, Cato saw flowers he had never seen before, and birds more colorful than anything he'd ever seen in the Forbidden Forest. As he tried not to think about how high above the world he was, Cato ascended the staircase to the palace.

Blue and red crystals encrusted the great doors, but here, where there was no danger, Cato saw no guards. At first he wondered if the palace was abandoned. Then he opened the doors wide and beheld the Goddess of Air, Valo.

Inside the Palace of Air, there were no boundaries. The chamber was open and wide and light poured through the chamber. Stained glass windows with magnificent pictures of peacocks and other majestic birds captured the light and sprayed a rainbow of color into the chamber.

Tiles were on the floor, and resting on the tiles were two large statues of Uta and Kide, and some ancient gods who he did not recognize because he had never even heard of them. If it had not been for his mysterious quest, he would never have seen Uta or Kide.

Beyond the statues was the goddess herself. She wore a golden robe that captured the light. Her hair was also as gold as the afternoon sun. Inside this great chamber, he faced the strongest of the goddesses, Valo. Like the other goddesses, she too stared at him, divining his thoughts, before speaking to him.

"Many men have tried and failed," said Valo. "Many men who thought they had faith. Men of faith, men of power, all have turned to smoke and vanished before my strength. But you are special. There is a beast inside of you that gives you strength, and I see a powerful heart pounding inside your chest. I would speak to you more. You may call me Valo, the Goddess of Air and Light."

"You may call me Cato, the one who was destined to free his people from the curse of the lion."

"These lions," wondered Valo. "I have had many lions for guardians. I used to have more. They are sacred to me. But I have not told you the whole story yet, and now is not the time. First you must tell me, where does your faith come from? Speak the truth."

Cato answered, "My faith comes from my people, for they have endured this curse for so long and yet they live in peace, tolerating the curse, not trying to fight it. My faith also comes from my strength as I complete these tasks to reclaim our humanity. But what gives me the strongest faith is the support and love of the precious woman I am in love with, the brave Princess Alzena. And this also gives me faith, and hope that you will tell me how to reclaim that humanity." He presented the locket to her, and slowly opened it with a click. Inside was Kide's hair, still ice blue. "I have the faith of your sister, Kide, as well. She asked me to present this to you. She said you would know."

The Goddess of Air was shocked at the present. She understood and dropped to one knee in reverence, inhaling sharply.

"No one has ever convinced Kide to part with even one strand of her magical hair," she said. "You must truly be the one who was destined to lift the curse if Kide has entrusted you with so many strands. Do you know what a rare gift this is? You must be a man of profound faith. It seems I must tell you everything that led up to this curse falling on your people. Before you undertake the final challenge, you have a right to know."

She swirled her hands through the air in a spiraling pattern. As she wove her magic, the air began to flow around her and grow dark and stormy as the air swirled. The column of smoke expanded to fill the room. Cato marveled at the strange cloud of smoke.

Inside the smoke, figures appeared, and the smoke cleared to reveal another world, one far above the earth, where goddesses and gods held court over the world of men. He had never seen this world before.

"This is the world of the gods, many years before your time."

Cato saw the god that the statue in the chamber was modeled after, pacing back and forth in the realm of the gods and goddesses with fury.

"That's my father there. His name is Ukko. He's one of the oldest sky gods. Once, many thousands of years ago, we goddesses and gods had control over you humans. But my father changed all that. He said that humanity was free to make its own decisions. The people were starving. They relied on the gods for everything and didn't know how to take care of themselves. Ukko understood he needed to set them free, so they could learn to farm and fish for themselves."

Cato saw a field with lions walking through it.

"These are my lions. They are my guardians. My evil sister used them against the humans."

Cato saw Valo's guardian lions roam the forest they protected. A woman in a red robe appeared through a portal.

"Varuni, she was my sister, but she hated my father for his ideas. She thought the humans were hers to control, and refused to relinquish her power."

Varuni began to pull some of the guardian lions towards her. She pulled them into the air, twisting their bodies with an evil spell until they became black, twisted monsters with many teeth that roared. Cato then saw these monsters attacking the humans.

As the smoke swirled around him, the scenery changed back to the world of the gods and goddesses. Cato saw Varuni and Ukko fighting and yelling at each other. Varuni's hands were balled up in fists of rage. Varuni was shaking her fist at Ukko.

Ukko cried out, "I told you, Varuni. Give up. The humans must have their freedom. You refuse to obey my commands. I have no choice but to banish you to the Forgotten Realm. It's too dangerous for you to be here, where you keep hurting the humans."

Varuni screamed with fury. "How dare you choose those foolish, bothersome humans, over me, your own daughter, the daughter of a god!"

Valo and Ukko cast a spell together, banishing her to the Forgotten Realm.

As she disappeared through the portal, Varuni cried, "I will have my revenge!"

Cato watched as the world changed again. Now only a faint shadow floated through the air.

"That's all she is now," said Valo. "Varuni's still weak. For now she can only speak and control people's minds, just as she always loved to do. But she is getting stronger. That's why you have to break the curse, to regain your power so you can fight her. Heed my warning, when a human vessel is weak, or saddened by grief, then she has the power to take over. Varuni could attack you when you least expect it. But you won't be alone. If she does break through, my sisters will be there. Call our names, and we will heed your call. For we have all seen that you have a special destiny, a future we have only hoped of."

Valo swirled her arms again, and the smoke curled up into a small column and twisted away into nothing.

"You have seen the power of air and learned of your destiny. But now you have a task to complete. Behind me, down that staircase, is the Hall of Mirrors. You must go and face your fears. With every fear you have ever defeated to get this far, you have defeated it by facing it head-on. In your final challenge, this is of the utmost importance. Whatever you do, don't stop looking at the mirror until you have seen everything it has to show you."

Cato asked, "Is there anything else you can tell me about what is coming?"

"Only that you must reach the end of the hall before the sun sets." Valo turned and pointed to a golden staircase behind her. Cato descended the staircase.

The Hall of Mirrors was the strangest place he had ever seen. Reflections of himself shone back from ever angle, from the mirrors on the floor, the mirrors on the ceiling, and the mirrors on each side of him. At the end of the hallway was an even larger mirror, but it was hanging on a door.

There were several mirrors between him and the door, but the distance looked impassable because of all the mirrors. Cato found himself disoriented. The mirrors on the floor were twisted, some making his face look bigger, and some making his head look tiny.

Inside the mirror to his side, he saw nothing. No reflection at all. He was very confused. He looked up and felt more disoriented as his body seemed to sway side to side in waves in the mirror above his head.

As he was trying to regain his balance, he saw the mirror under his feet cave in and he fell backwards. Expecting the mirror behind him to hit him in the back and catch him, he shouted as he continued falling, as if the mirror had turned to liquid behind him.

He hit the floor, rolled over, expecting a mirror, but was shocked to discover dirt and rocks beneath him.

Chapter Twenty-Five

The Lions' Realm

Still trying to figure out how he had ended up on the ground after being in a hall of mirrors miles above the world, Cato looked upwards, about to get on his feet, and saw clear blue sky above him. He tried to get up, but as he looked around him he found himself rooted to the spot and decided it was best to stay there.

Dozens of lions surrounded Cato, padding about and staring at him viciously. There was no humanity in them at all. They were far bigger than Cato's lion form ever became. He recognized the lions as Valo's guardians. Between their bodies, he caught glimpses of a green plain.

The lions began talking to one another about Cato.

"What are we going to do with him?" one asked out loud.

"How did he get into our realm?" asked another.

"Why did he come here?" asked a third.

The largest lion there, the leader, spoke then, and all the others fell silent. "Wait! I know who he is. That is Cato, one of the Lion-People, the ones our brothers and sisters were tied to with a powerful spell so many years ago. I had almost forgotten about them." He was a very old lion, so old his hair had turned silver and his face was scarred from hundreds of years of guarding the Goddess of Air.

"Cato, why did you come here?" asked the leader.

"To break the curse that binds my people to the lions, that forces us to turn into lions every night against our will. I came here to break that curse."

The leader looked sagely and solemnly at Cato. "Cato, I cannot allow you to leave the lion realm. It has been foretold that if the curse was ever lifted, Varuni would return in fury and kill us all. I cannot allow you to leave and let my people be killed."

Cato looked back at the leader, trying to look bold, and answered. "I don't believe that prophecy will ever come true. Princess Alzena of the realm of Santara has found a way to save you. I have already overcome two of the trials to lift this curse. If I don't finish this trial by sundown, I'm going to fail my quest and I'll never be able to destroy Varuni, the one that we know of as the Evil Sorceress. Just let me complete my trial!"

The leader looked suspiciously at Cato. "I don't trust you. I can't risk the lives of my pride." Then he turned to the other lions. "Take him away to a cage where he can't endanger us anymore."

Cato shook with fear. Now, so close to the end of his quest, he realized that he was still capable of failing.

Two large lions came over to Cato, and grabbed his shoulders in their jaws. They dragged him to a dark cave where they lived, and put him in a wooden cage. Cato, his hands wrapped in vines, was tied to one of the branches to keep his hands behind his back. As he struggled to get free, the leader glared at him. He tried to beg.

"Please, set me free," begged Cato. "I must complete my task while the sun is still in the sky."

The leader snarled at Cato. "Why should I trust you?" he sneered. "You know I want my brothers returned home. Don't punish me with idle promises."

Cato answered, "They're not idle. I came here to bring your people home. As soon as the curse is lifted, I will end Varuni's reign of terror."

"You promise freedom. But we are growing weaker by the day. For too long we have waited for our brethren."

Cato continued to struggle against the vines as he was talking, and finally managed to squirm his way to where Uta's weapon was still attached to his side, looking like any other tool a human might carry. He grabbed the weapon in his hand, and was able to command it to change at his will. He closed his eyes and said, "Fire!"

The weapon became a burning sword. All the lions turned to him in fear. Cato quickly set fire to the branches of the cage and as they burned he was able to roll clear because fire was not one of the things he feared. He broke through the burning branches, and once he was free of the cage, the vines were no longer holding him hostage. He pulled his hands free and swung his sword around in a great circle. All the lions backed away, retreating in fear.

"All I want is my freedom!" cried Cato. "I promise if you let me go, no harm will come to any of you and your brothers will return home!"

The leader spoke to him. "Promise me you will stop Varuni from ever hurting us again."

"I will do everything in my power to help you. I will reunite you with your brothers. You have my solemn word."

The leader turned to the other lions. "Let him pass! If he thinks he can stop Varuni, there's no harm in letting him try."

Cato left the cave and returned to the open plain. The mirror was solid, and he thought he would be trapped there forever. He pushed hard against it over and over again, but the door would not release. Finally, he pushed the right place and was sucked through. He found himself once again in the Hall of Mirrors. Cato tried to regain his balance as he tried to get used to the crazy angles and strange reflections again. He heard voices whispering to him from every side. Fear attacked him from every angle.

"Your princess is dead!"

"You failed the challenge!"

"You won't be able to free anyone!"

Cato stumbled, but shook his head violently and pushed the voices out of his mind, crying out, "I will not fail! And I would know if the love of my life was dead. You cannot fool me. Voices cannot hurt me."

The voices faded, and Cato relaxed and went back to the task of staring into the mirrors. He looked into the mirror beside him. This time, instead of the strange empty space confronting him before, he saw trees. He saw his house in the Forbidden Forest, and his mother Lena crying in agony. A baby lion was being born, a baby that Cato realized was himself. As he kept watching the scene, it faded away and Cato knew he could continue. He walked to the next mirror.

Cato saw himself as a young boy, enduring his transformation to a lion for the first time. He screamed in pain. As he watched himself in the mirror, he forced himself to keep looking, to not turn away. Once the transformation was complete, the image slowly dissolved.

In another mirror, Cato saw the first time he carved a piece of wood. He looked back fondly at the smile on his face as he admired his handiwork. He saw his mother standing over him and smiling approvingly. Happy that this was a good memory, Cato watched as the scene dissolved.

In the next mirror, Cato saw his father. As his father was being killed, he screamed in panic and the life went out of his eyes. Cato used all of his strength to force himself to keep watching. Once the blood stopped flowing, the scene finally dissolved.

Within the next mirror, Cato saw the first time he ever ventured into the forest far enough to discover Masala's village. He remembered the surprise at seeing lions in broad daylight, and watched as the people of the village accepted him with open arms. Then the scene dissolved.

In the last mirror, Cato witnessed the first time he had ever met Alzena, in the marketplace with the cloudberries rolling around. Just watching her in the mirror made his heart skip a beat. As the scene changed to show the first time they had kissed, he felt his heart overflowing with love and happiness.

As he turned to reach the next mirror, he found himself at the end of the hallway.

"Cato!" cried a voice behind him. He turned. The goddess Valo stood in the hallway, bathed in white light.

"All the tasks have been completed," said Valo. "You have finally faced your fears. The lions can now leave your people and return home."

Valo placed her hand on his head, and magic energy flowed through him. Cato dropped to his knees and roared as the separation began. As the magic went through his body, he felt as if his muscles were being seared from his bones with burning flames. Bones crunched and snapped and were magically healed again, skin ripped, and tissue tore, as the lion and the human were finally separated after being cursed for so long.

The lion, finally separate from Cato's body, took one final look of farewell and dove through the mirror. On the other side, his brothers and sisters were waiting for him. They all smiled and walked away, leaving nothing in the mirror but the open plain.

Valo led Cato out of the Hall of Mirrors back to the great chamber.

Once he was back in the chamber with Uta and Kide waiting already, Valo spoke to him again.

"You are free now, Cato. The curse has been lifted forever. Prince Eino left his cloak behind when Varuni turned him into a Lion-Person. It has been here ever since, a reminder of his lost humanity. Now that you set the Lion-People free, you have the right to wear Prince Eino's cloak." She put the cloak over his shoulders. "Lintu will return you to Santara now. Go in peace."

Cato grabbed the rope on the side of the saddle to pull himself up, and as the great bird flew away from the palace, Cato saw lion after lion, one by one, ascending the golden stairs of the palace and returning home. His eyes blurred with tears of joy as they flew away from the palace.

Chapter Twenty-Six

Varuni

As Cato flew down from the clouds, he saw Santara spread out below him. As Lintu continued to descend, he saw the volcano getting closer and closer. They flew down through the air until they were near the ground. Cato saw Alzena's bright battle armor and her flaming red hair and recognized her immediately.

He tugged on the bird's reins. She swooped down to the ground and landed gracefully. Cato jumped off the bird and came across the field to meet Alzena. As he approached her, he paused. In that moment, Alzena's eyes turned blood red. Cato realized what was happening and backed away in revulsion, unable to separate the creature possessing Alzena from the woman he cared about "Alzena!" he cried.

Alzena smiled menacingly at him. "Now you'll never have her again!" she laughed in a deep voice.

"I know you can hear me, Alzena," said Cato. "I'm not giving up on you!"

Varuni laughed again, dangerously. "Now I will take what is mine! I will control you and everyone here forever!" She drew a sharp blade from her thigh and stabbed Cato in his right arm before he could draw it back. When the blade struck him, he knew that Alzena was completely gone. He saw a shield on the nearby horse, so he ran over to grab it to use to defend himself. Putting the shield between him and Alzena, he roared in pain. She kept stabbing at the shield over and over again, screaming in fury. "Alzena!" he cried out loudly. "Get control of yourself! I know you can hear me in there! Alzena! Fight it! Fight back, Alzena! Let our love become your strength!"

Deep inside her mind, Alzena was chained to a chair. Far away, like echoes on the wind, she heard Cato's voice calling out to her.

"Cato!" she cried out, though her voice was weak. She listened carefully. The wind carried his voice away, and then brought it back again.

"Fight back!" There was a long silence. Then, far away, she heard, "Let our love become your strength!"

Unable to move, Alzena closed her eyes and thought about Cato, the powerful man that she had fallen in love with, the man who'd kept her safe and warm when she was in the forest surrounded by wild beasts. As she focused on him, her heart began to pound faster. She felt power returning to her.

Her blood boiled and she struggled mightily against the chains. With her newfound strength, the chains snapped and she was free of the chair.

Varuni stopped stabbing and paused with the spear above her head. She looked confused. Cato felt a surge of relief as he saw the goddess Valo appear behind the possessed Alzena and push her way into her body, vanishing like a cloud. As she entered, Alzena dropped her hands and a black mist poured out of her mouth. Cato backed away. It formed upon the ground into an ugly, blackened creature, twisted and distorted. The woman who was once a beautiful goddess was now a freakish monster. She was defending herself with a long spear.

"You thought breaking the curse was going to stop me?" Varuni growled. "This time all you miserable humans will die. You've failed this time, sister! I will start anew, destroy everything and leave nothing in my wake but mindless creatures that will serve me forever!" Varuni started chanting, beginning to cast the destructive spell.

Cato dropped the shield, grabbed his weapon from his side, and screamed "Fire sword!" He brandished the huge fiery sword and lunged for Varuni. She tried to fight him off, raking the sword with her claws, but Cato was faster and smarter. He continued to fight her, avoiding her blows.

Cato saw Kide appear on the battlefield and become a huge polar bear. Uta also arrived, and became a powerful firebird. Together, they attacked Varuni relentlessly, the firebird tearing her with its talons and breathing fire as Varuni screamed and fought back. The polar bear lunged at her and mangled her legs, tearing her blackened flesh from her bones with gigantic paws.

Valo separated from Alzena to help her sisters, and Alzena fell to the ground, shaking and twisting. Valo became a powerful white lion with piercing blue eyes, and she also attacked Varuni relentlessly. As she bit through Varuni's flesh, the light seared her body, and she screamed.

In spite of their efforts, she continued to try to cast the spell. They looked at each other and knew what they needed to do.

They became powerful elemental forces—fire, water, and air poured upon

Varuni at once. The flames seared Varuni to her very soul, wrapping around her skin. Water thundered over her and she fell to the ground. A huge ice storm covered her and she began to freeze. As she tried to melt the ice with her hands, lighting from Valo struck her repeatedly, binding her hands with electricity. As she froze solid, she dropped the spear and it rolled away.

However, she was still able to summon power from the earth. Strange black beetles rose out of the ground and began to swarm around. Cato slashed them away with his sword, and he noticed that Alzena was lying on the ground and writhing in pain. As the beetles began to clear away, significantly reduced by the fire sword, he rushed over to see if she was all right.

As Alzena writhed, she cried out, "Cato, now! Use Varuni's spear! Aim for her chest!"

Cato saw that Varuni was frozen for the moment, but could break free at any second. She continued to fight the elemental forces that surrounded her. She chanting, still trying desperately to cast the spell. The goddesses had managed to keep Varuni distracted and she did not notice her spear on the ground. He knew that it was now or never.

Cato ran over and grabbed the weapon. As he ran for her, she broke free of the ice and began to chant louder, so obsessed with it that she didn't see Cato approach. He stabbed as hard as he could, impaling her all the way through her heart.

As she began to die, the face of the Goddess Varuni emerged briefly, and for a moment, she regained her former beauty and glory. Varuni shone with inner light, a true goddess once again.

The goddesses continued to sap her power.

Screaming, Varuni began to glow with a strange inner light that broke through her skin. She screamed one last time and vanished, the ball of light engulfing her body.

Cato saw the goddesses surrounding her all becoming one power, swirling into each other. A great portal appeared before Varuni, and as Cato watched, she was pulled inside, stretching and being sucked through. The elemental goddesses remained where they were, slowly returning to their divine forms.

The three stood before him on the plain where Varuni had finally been defeated.

"We couldn't have done it without you, Cato. Now Varuni has been banished to a place where she can never escape. The world we have sent her to has no exits. She can never leave."

"I don't know how I can ever repay you. I'm forever in your debt."

"Worship us again."

Cato turned away then, knowing Varuni was finally gone.

He ran back over to Alzena and held her head in his hands. "Alzena, wake up, my love!"

Alzena opened her eyes, which were blue again. "What happened?" she asked. "Is everyone all right?"

Cato answered, "You were taken over by powers beyond your control. But it's all over now. The curse has finally been lifted. We're free, my love."

Chapter Twenty-Seven

The Wedding

Cato and Alzena stood on the battlefield, looking at each other in wonder. "Lintu will take you back to the Forbidden Forest now," said Valo.

Cato and Alzena got on the back of the bird, using the ropes, and Lintu flew across the forests and fields, past the marketplace and the palace, and finally to the Forbidden Forest, as Alzena watched in wide-eyed amazement. She had never been on the back of a bird before.

Cato was not prepared, as he dismounted and helped Alzena to the ground, for the sight of all the Lion-People slowly emerging from the forest. His heart lifted in joy as Lena emerged first, blinking her eyes. He noticed that she looked completely different. Her eyes were blue and her whiskers were gone. She stood tall and proud, no longer shy and hunched like an animal. As the other people of his tribe began to emerge, all of them human now, he was overjoyed.

"He's the one who lifted the curse," said Lena, pointing at Cato.

All the people ran over to Cato, hugging him, lifting him up on their shoulders and cheering, lifting Alzena up as well.

Cato spoke with pride and conviction after they had set them down again. "I am the one who set you free from this curse, but not without the help of many gods and goddesses. You are now free to travel through this beautiful kingdom of Santara, this place which was once ours, without judgment or fear."

All his people bowed before him. Cato turned and got down on one knee in front of Alzena.

"In front of all my people, Princess Alzena, I have just one favor to ask of you."

Alzena looked at him, surprised that he would want anything at all after his victory. "Anything you ask, Cato, but if I was stronger, Varuni would never have possessed me," she answered.

"Princess Alzena, from the moment I saw you, I knew that you were special. But you have become the greatest woman I have ever met. You found a way for me to lift this curse, you helped me destroy the evil sorceress Varuni, and you never stopped believing in me. I want to spend the rest of my life with you. Alzena, will you marry me?"

Alzena had tears in her eyes. "Absolutely," she cried, and a great cheer went up among Cato's people.

Inside the church, hundreds of people had gathered. The entire royal family was there, along with visiting nobles. On Cato's side sat every one of the Lion-People, smiling and no longer persecuted. Behind the altar where Cato stood was a stained glass image of the Goddess of Light, and as the light shone through the panes, it danced across the floor in many colors and landed on Princess Alzena.

The wedding dress made her look like a goddess herself, covered in thousands of beads and draped in lace, as she walked to the front of the church, led by Queen Lydia, dressed in the finest royal dress, which bore the swan as its design, held her head high, choking back tears of pride and carefully wiping her eyes.

Cato could hardly recognize Alzena anymore, because the woman in front of him was not the lady in the marketplace he had met.

The leader of the church stood in front of the altar, and as Cato and Alzena looked at each other, smiling, he spoke. "Today we are gathered to witness, before the Goddess of Light, the marriage of Princess Alzena and Prince Cato. Do you, Prince Cato, savior of the Lion-People, take Princess Alzena to be your wife, the mother of your children, to have and to hold, so long as you both may live?"

"I do," answered Cato. He took a deep breath to compose himself, but tears of joy escaped his eyes.

"And do you, Princess Alzena, you who found a way to set the Lion-People free from the curse, do you promise to take Prince Cato as your husband, to love and to cherish, to have and to hold, so long as you both shall live?"

"I do," answered Alzena, beaming. The smile meant even more to Cato than her words, and he knew his eyes were beaming as well.

"Is there anything you wish to say to Cato?" asked the church leader.

"Before the Goddess of Light, I will love you from now until eternity. Everything I am and everything I have is now yours."

"What would you like to say to Alzena?" he asked Cato.

Cato answered, "I have loved you since the first time I saw you and I will love you until my last breath. What's mine is yours as well. What was once the Forbidden Forest is now open for all the people of Santara to enjoy." He picked up the ring from the waiting pillow and put it on Alzena's shaking finger. Alzena picked up the other ring and carefully placed it on Cato's finger, but her hands were still shaking.

"These rings are a symbol of Cato and Alzena's love and commitment to each other. You may now kiss the bride."

As Cato kissed Alzena, she felt flooded with radiant light, and as their lips parted, she felt completely freed of any fear or nightmares. She stared deeply into Cato's eyes. She hardly heard the church leader as he said, "May I now present Prince Cato and Princess Alzena, husband and wife." Even when the crowd began to cheer, she barely heard the roar, because she was still lost in Cato's eyes.

The wedding feast was massive, laid out on many tables for all the guests. Everybody was happily eating and laughing and talking.

A dancer and a singer walked into the hall. Dressed in clothes from another land, bright squares of color, they carried joy in their bodies. "We have come to sing and dance for you," they said. The singer sang a haunting, sweet song with a voice as soft as silver. As the dancer moved across the floor in a complicated waltz, the guests were mesmerized.

"Where do you hail from?" asked Prince Cato.

"We come from the Land of the Musaat, where all the great artists and thinkers are inspired."

"That was the most wonderful dance I've ever seen, and the song was amazing. You must perform for us again sometime" said Cato.

"Indeed we will." They answered as one and left the hall.

"Enjoy the feast," declared Cato. As everyone sat down to eat, Cato looked at his new wife and didn't want to be at the feast anymore. He ate enough to be polite, but Alzena was gazing back at him, so before long, she pushed her plate away as well. He took Alzena by the hand and they left the feast to be alone.

They went to the hill overlooking the kingdom, where they had talked many days ago. As before, Cato could see the harbor and the mountains and the forest, but after his great adventure, the world seemed a little smaller somehow.

Alzena gripped his hand tighter. "All this is yours now, Cato."

Cato returned her grasp. "No," he answered her. "It's ours."

They turned towards each other to kiss as the two moons shone above them.

About the Author

Melissa Saari

Melissa Saari lives in Washington State where the Columbia River, the river that powers America, rushes near her front door, and every summer, smoke from forest fires fill the sky. These powerful elements inspire her writing, whether it's romance, fantasy, or horror.

Melissa also has two loving, protective dogs: a female pit bull named Marla and a male Chow called Leo. Her dogs provide comedy, therapy, and inspiration for her stories.

Melissa will always be a writer. She begins her Master's Degree in Screenwriting this fall to study the complex film industry and how her vision can be shared with billions of moviegoers.